Mists of Danger

B.J. Hoff

ACCENT BOOKS
Denver, Colorado

The town of Red Oak, Alabama, and the Colony of the Lotus are fictional. The characters and events in this story are creations of the author's imagination and no resemblance to any persons living or dead is intended.

ACCENT BOOKS

A division of Accent Publications, Inc.
12100 West Sixth Avenue
P.O. Box 15337
Denver, Colorado 80215

Library of Congress Catalog Card Number 86-70567

ISBN 0-89636-206-X

This book is dedicated to the memory of
William M. Simon,
my father—and "a good cop."

Author's Note

My sincere thanks to the Alabama State Chamber of Commerce and the Alabama Department of Economic and Community Affairs for their generous assistance.

A faith that lives
in a heart that loves—
This can change the world....

1

Danni St. John squinted nervously into the distorted rainy night. Her eyes involuntarily followed the hypnotic sweep of the Celica's windshield wipers. The scene in front of her was uncomfortably like something out of an Edgar Allan Poe story. She half-expected to see a screeching raven swoop down from one of the enormous old oak trees which lined the dark, deserted streets. The car radio provided a mindless background noise.

She leveled her glasses on the narrow bridge of her nose and applied a bit more pressure to the accelerator, ignoring the apprehension that had been building inside her for the past hour. But a treacherous combination of soggy leaves and wet pavement caused the car to unexpectedly fishtail and turn almost sideways in the middle of the street. She couldn't stop a small cry of frightened surprise as she slithered to a stop.

At the same time, a sharp gust of wind roared through the trees flanking the street, forcing their limbs almost to the ground. Danni stared straight ahead, stunned and wide-eyed with alarm as a dazzling bolt of lightning hurled itself directly in front of her, bathing Montgomery Street in an eerie luminescence.

She swallowed hard, nearly choking on what felt like an oversized wad of cotton lodged in her throat. Her hands were cold and clammy on the steering wheel, and she wiped them on her jeans clad legs a couple of times. Finally, after a long moment and a short prayer, she smiled at her own skittishness.

"Lovely night for a murder," she mumbled, peering from

side to side into the darkness outside the car. "Just so long as it isn't mine." Already tired to the point of exhaustion, her nerves were tightly strung from fighting the relentless, driving rain for the last hundred miles.

She checked the rearview mirror, then slowly righted the car, cautiously inching ahead. The welcoming blink of colored lights just ahead on her left brought a sigh of relief. She increased her speed a little, eager to find a place where she could get out of the rain, stretch her legs, and get specific directions to the Colony. Her anticipation grew even keener when she saw that the multi-colored lights belonged to Ferguson's Twenty-Four Hour Service Stop. Ray Ferguson had been on that corner for as long as she could remember.

But she hadn't been back to Red Oak for almost five years. The last time she'd come home had been for her father's funeral. Afterward she had helped her mother sell the florist shop and pack for her move to Florida, where she now shared a condo with Danni's Aunt Kathryn. She wondered how many other landmarks might have remained untouched. Red Oak was a small town of no more than ten thousand people that had never seemed to catch up with the growth and change taking place in many other areas throughout the state of Alabama. In fact, Danni would have been genuinely surprised by any major changes in the town where she'd been born and raised. She had always assumed that the placid, yawning little farm community nestled in the northern part of the state would somehow remain as it had been for over seventy-five years.

Her recent spurt of cheerfulness abruptly fled when she saw the lights at Ferguson's go black. *So much for twenty-four hour service*, she thought cynically. Her sense of expectation quickly changed to anxiety when she realized that the entire block was dark. Even the street lights were out.

She drove slowly through an intersection, now without a

traffic light, and turned left into the service station. Another sharp flash of lightning provided just enough illumination for her to catch a glimpse of four white-robed figures appearing from the side of a white van parked at the pumps, moving quickly to the shelter of the brick building's overhang.

Danni very nearly panicked. She was halfway onto the blacktop of the station's corner lot when she slammed on the brakes. The momentum threw her forward against the steering wheel and she avoided by mere inches the metal railing at the north end of the lot.

She had never been a cowardly person. The considerable success she presently enjoyed as a journalist and an editor hadn't been achieved by being timid. But the sour taste of fear now tightened her mouth. She was, after all, alone on a deserted street in the middle of an Alabama rainstorm, with no lights and no one in sight to help her.

With an unsteady hand, she wiped a thin line of perspiration from her forehead, darting an anxious glance into the rearview mirror. Her sense of logic seemed frozen. She couldn't decide whether to stay or try for a fast retreat. Vaguely, as though echoing up from a dark chamber, the calming voice of the radio announcer penetrated the silence, and Danni noted absently that the music she'd been listening to had given way to a news broadcast. She found the smooth male voice oddly inappropriate for her present situation, then expelled a sigh of impatience with herself for giving her emotions such loose rein. Her attention sharpened when she heard the Colony mentioned.

" . . . Reverend Ra, administrator of the Colony of the Lotus, stated that Mr. Kendrick had apparently suffered from a variety of heart problems for some time. As a guest of the Colony, he will be provided with the traditional interment ceremony afforded to those persons who are without known living relatives."

When the station resumed the music format, Danni

turned off the radio, feeling as though she were suspended in some sort of crazy time warp. So intent was she on resisting the fear threatening to overwhelm her that she didn't notice the approach of one of the white specters until it tapped lightly on her car window. Danni choked off a scream, pressing a clenched fist against her mouth as she stared in disbelief at the nodding apparition on the other side of the glass.

The face peering in at her was almost as white as the hooded garment enveloping it and frightfully misshapen by the rivulets of water cascading down the car window. Danni's mind spun crazily and she couldn't remember whether or not her doors were locked. For one insane moment she had the gruesome thought that she might be about to provide the next obituary announcement for the radio station.

Danni dropped her gaze to the blue insignia on the left shoulder of the garment the creature outside her window was wearing—a lotus imposed upon the outline of a pyramid with a pseudo-Egyptian drawing of a hawk just underneath it. However, it wasn't until the bearded young man in the hooded rain poncho spoke that she felt the first hint of understanding begin to surface.

"Ma'am? Are you all right?"

Danni stared at him blankly, then looked from the emblem on his poncho to the van, seeing the same insignia minus the hawk painted on the side of the vehicle. Feeling somewhat foolish and embarrassed, she loosened her rigid grip on the steering wheel. Allowing her shoulders to slump with the welcome release of tension, she also relaxed her jaw from the vise it had been clamped in since she'd first spotted the white figures. Finally she was able to attempt a weak smile.

The young man outside her window studied her with apparently genuine concern. "Ma'am—can we be of any help to you?"

Her fear gave way to relief as she pushed her glasses up into her hair, their usual resting place. She lowered the car window.

"I'm sorry—I—you startled me. The lights went out . . . and then I saw you . . . and I thought . . . . " She let her voice drift off into the cold, damp air outside.

"Are you having car trouble?"

"No—no, I just wanted to get out of the rain and get some directions." Her mind cleared even more. "You're from the Colony?"

"Yes, ma'am." His youthful smile was guileless, almost beatific.

"Then you *can* help me. I need directions so I can drive out there first thing in the morning."

His smile brightened even more. "You're joining us?"

Stuck for an appropriate answer, Danni considered her reply carefully. "Well—in a way. Listen, let me park and then maybe you can draw me a rough map, if you don't mind."

He stepped aside, watching Danni as she pulled up and parked at the side of the building. Before getting out of the car, she pulled on a blue quilted jacket and tucked her hair inside the hood.

The fair young man with the blond beard reached for her hand to help her from the car, continuing to hold onto her as they dashed for the shelter of the building. The three young people huddling there wore matching white ponchos with the blue emblem, and each of them turned a somewhat vacuous smile on Danni as she stepped beneath the overhang.

She glanced at them curiously, flashing a quick, sincere grin. "Is the station closed?"

"It looks like it," replied the only girl in the group. She was extremely pretty, with shy green eyes and black shining hair

11

peeping out from the border of her hood. "Do you think Mr. Ferguson is ill, Brother Penn?" Her question was directed to the young man who had first approached Danni.

"He probably closed up because of all the power losses we've had tonight," the youth replied, turning to Danni to explain. "The storm has knocked out the power two or three times so far—all over town—even as far out as the Colony. Fortunately, we have our own auxiliary generators."

One of the other boys spoke up. "We brought the van in to get gas and have a tire replaced," he said, looking at Danni. "Do you live here in town, ma'am?"

"She's coming to the Colony tomorrow," the young man referred to as Brother Penn informed them with a smile.

Danni quickly guessed all of them to be teenagers, positive the girl couldn't be more than sixteen and reasonably sure that the tall, lanky Brother Penn was the oldest in the group, perhaps nineteen. He was the only one who wasn't clean-shaven, and the only one who wore the emblem of the hawk underneath the Colony logo. *They're just kids,* she thought. Her facial expression didn't reveal the hot stab of anger she felt, anger that she quickly dismissed, knowing she couldn't afford it. Emotional detachment—as much as humanly possible—was going to be absolutely essential for what she had to do, and it had to begin right now.

"I'm sorry," she said warmly, "I haven't even introduced myself. I'm Danni St. John. I'll be working at the Colony with the newspaper. I'm the new editor."

The girl was the first to speak, extending her hand to Danni. "I'm Sister Lann," she said shyly. "This is Brother Penn." She nodded to the boy on her left who flashed that same vacant smile that for some reason was beginning to irritate Danni. *I must really be uptight,* she thought dryly, *when a smile gets under my skin.*

"And I'm Brother Rudd," chimed the short, apple-cheeked

boy directly across from Danni. "This is Brother Hall—he's my life brother as well." His voice was high, almost childish.

Danni assumed he meant that the taller, dull-eyed youth standing beside him was his natural brother.

"The Colony's easy to find," said Brother Penn, who seemed to be the acknowledged leader of the group. "All you have to do is drive out of town on 72 for about five miles, then turn right at the old Suter Foundry on Dead End Road. But you said you weren't coming until morning. Where are you staying tonight?"

"My home is here. That is, it used to be," Danni explained. "My mother lives in Florida now. Some friends of our family rented our house until just a few weeks ago, but they moved out of state. So the house is mine to use, at least for now."

The girl looked skeptical. "Don't you think maybe you should just follow us out to the Colony tonight, instead of staying in town alone, with the power being out and all?"

"Oh, no, I'll be fine," Danni protested with a smile. "I've really been looking forward to getting home again, you know?" And so she had. She could hardly wait to get unpacked, have a hot shower, and plop down on the high four-poster bed in her old bedroom.

"If you like," Brother Penn said agreeably, "give us a time, and one of us will meet you at your house in the morning, so you can follow us to the Colony."

"Well—" Danni hesitated, caught offguard by their eagerness to help her.

"It won't be any trouble," he quickly assured her. "What street is your house on?"

"De Soto Drive. It's the last house on the right—a white two-story. That is, it *was* white; I suppose it might have been repainted by now. The number's eighteen-ten."

"Will nine o'clock be all right?" he asked. "We have to be

at the bus station by eight-fifteen to meet some guests. We could swing by for you afterward."

"Great! Listen, I really appreciate this. I was a little worried about finding the Colony, since it wasn't here when I left . . . . "

Danni was too involved in her conversation with the teens to notice that a darkened car, parked no more than a block away from them, was slowly easing out from the curb. She and the others whirled around in unison when it suddenly roared to life. Its glaring headlights blinded them as red spotlights blazed, throwing eerie, colored shadows against the darkness, while the piercing scream of a siren shattered the night.

"What—" Her half-formed question died on her lips as the car gunned forward. It lunged wildly onto the pavement of the service station like some sort of metal monster gone mad, then cut directly in front of the white-clad huddle surrounding Danni before screeching to a dead halt.

Danni stared open-mouthed at the howling phantom. Her face paled and she felt her pulse banging in her ears as the door of a patrol car flew open and a dark giant of a man stepped outside.

2

Behind her, Danni heard Brother Penn groan softly, then mumble, "McGarey."

"The sheriff," Sister Lann whispered, touching Danni lightly on the shoulder.

Danni stared with undisguised interest at the khaki-clad figure approaching. From some distant place in her memory a buzz of faint recognition sounded, quickly lost in her stunned appraisal of the man striding toward them.

Her first impression had been accurate. He was a giant. Of course, most men over five-ten seemed tall to Danni when viewed from her full height of five-foot-two. Still, this one had to be at least an intimidating six-four. With shoulders broad enough to gracefully balance his height and an expanse of chest that would make most Olympic swimmers look positively wimpy, he was no less than overwhelming.

As the black-bearded giant roughly parted the huddle and injected himself directly in front of her, Danni, too dazed to realize she was staring rudely, tilted her head back enough to allow for a better view. She removed her glasses as her hood fell away from her tousled, wheat-colored hair. Her gaze traveled upward from a dark leather jacket with a badge, past a thick, jet-black beard and mustache, then on to deep brown eyes that were appraising her every bit as boldy as she was him. He wasn't wearing a hat, and his sable hair, worn long enough to fall casually forward on each side of his forehead, glistened with raindrops.

Danni's instincts told her this big, somewhat menacing man towering over her wouldn't even begin to fit the types of southern law officers with whom she was familiar. She had worked with a number of policemen, but something about this sheriff put her immediately on edge.

Danni found his frowning stare more than a little unnerving but managed a weak smile, puzzled by a glint of what appeared to be surprise in his expression. She was confused when she noticed that his frown seemed to hold more concern than hostility.

"Do you have a problem here, young lady?" His voice was unexpectedly soft, with that sweet-flowing, unhurried drawl unique to Alabama men.

Danni had almost forgotten what a pleasurable experience it could be, listening to a gentle, creamy-rich baritone make an endearment out of "y'all" and a two-syllable word out of "here."

"Problem?" With dismay, she heard her voice break into a thin, childish squeak. "Oh—no, no problem!"

If it hadn't been such a ridiculous notion, she would have thought the man looked disappointed. Brushing aside the unreasonable idea, she watched him survey the group of young people with a hard, deliberate gaze that aroused almost defensive feelings for them.

Looking directly at Brother Penn, he spoke softly but in a blatantly sarcastic tone. "I s'pose there's a real good reason for you all to be standing out here in the rain this late at night?"

"Why, yes, Sheriff," the young man replied evenly. "We were hoping to get a new tire and put some gas in the van. But Mr. Ferguson has apparently gone home."

Turning his gaze back to Danni, the sheriff moved closer in an attempt to get under the shelter of the overhang. His dark hair now hung wetly around his face, emphasizing deep-set, disturbing eyes and high, firmly molded cheekbones that hinted of an Indian ancestor somewhere in his background. "And you are—?" He let the question hang.

"Danni St. John," she replied quickly.

16

"You're with these people, ma'am?" Danni thought his words held an edge of distaste, and wondered if it were directed at her or the members of the Colony. For some unexplainable reason she didn't want to be the target of his disapproval.

"Uh—well, not really. That is, I am now, but I—"

Sister Lann interrupted. "Miss St. John is the new editor of the *Peace Standard*, Sheriff McGarey. And she used to live here."

Danni sensed the sudden sharpening of his interest, and she began to feel uncomfortably like a bug under glass as he scrutinized her.

"Editor?" A muscle at his right eye twitched, and Danni thought he was close to smirking. "Well, now, it must be darker than I thought," he drawled. "I wouldn't have taken you to be old enough for a high-class job like that." He crossed his arms over his chest and waited for her reaction.

I don't like you either, cowboy, she thought, suddenly infuriated with his overbearing, macho attitude. "I can assure you that I'm perfectly qualified, Sheriff," she replied tartly.

His expression didn't alter. "St. John? Any relation to the folks that used to own the florist shop?"

"My parents," she said cooly, meeting his gaze. "I'm a native." She watched him carefully for any change, thinking he might back off a little once he realized she had a right to be in what he obviously considered *his* town.

"Mm-hmm." And that, apparently, summed up his opinion of Danni and her parents.

After a long moment, during which he looked around to give her car a thorough appraisal, he turned back to her. "You're stayin' out at the . . . Colony, ma'am?"

Danni didn't miss the slight emphasis on the word *Colony*. Puzzled, she tilted her head to one side, raising her hand to wipe away the raindrops which were falling from her hair onto her cheeks. "No. I'll be staying at my home—my parents' place. On De Soto."

He nodded. "The white two-story with the little greenhouse in back."

"That's right."

"No one's lived there for a few weeks," he said in a matter-of-fact tone. "It'll be cold—and you won't have any lights."

A lot you care, she thought acidly. "I'll be fine," she said sweetly through clenched teeth.

He shrugged. "Your choice." Again he studied her, lowering his arms from his chest to push one hand into his back pocket.

Suddenly it hit Danni full force, the memory that had been teasing her since he'd stepped out of the patrol car. *Logan McGarey!* Yes ... it *had* to be him! The high school football star who had gone off to Vietnam and returned as a highly decorated war hero. *Of course!*

For a moment she saw herself many years before. She'd been a skinny, unimpressive little flute player with the Red Oak Middle School Band, marching proud-as-a-peacock in her red and white uniform down the football field in a special half-time show, a combination effort with the high school for the homecoming game.

She'd been no more than twelve then, and Logan McGarey a distant senior and quarterback of the varsity football team. He had made local football history that night by staking his claim to the field and leading Red Oak to a stunning victory over their traditional rival from Scottsboro. They had captured the state championship for the first time in fifteen years, and in the process gave the name of McGarey its first real touch of respectability.

The McGareys had been tenant farmers. Theirs had been a big family—lots of kids, Danni remembered. And they'd been poor, extremely poor. The family didn't have a very good reputation either, she dimly recalled. Hadn't one of Logan's brothers died in prison? There had been some sort of scandal, she was certain, but she couldn't remember the circumstances.

Strange, she thought, *that the memory of that magic, late-autumn night was still so vivid, even after all these years.* Danni had fallen in love that night for the first time, watching the dark giant with the thick black hair control the football field in what appeared to be the result of both genius and awesome physical prowess.

Bits and pieces of old memories rushed at Danni. He'd attended her church for awhile, too, she suddenly remembered. He had been tall and too thin at that time—a far cry from the big man now standing in front of her with the look of a professional athlete, as well as a definite air of self-confident power. Back then, his clothes had never seemed to fit him, and they were nearly always worn-out. He had been the only one of his large family who came to church—at least, the only one who came to Danni's church.

Her mother had commented on that once, expressing sympathy for him. "You have to give him credit, coming by himself all the time, as he does. And he must feel so awkward, in those worn-out clothes he has to wear. He's always alone," Nancy St. John had clucked sadly. "I've never seen the boy with another soul."

Danni had forgotten about him, of course, once he'd graduated and gone on to Vietnam. Even when he'd returned from his stint there, widely touted by a number of state newspapers for his heroism, she'd been too involved in her own whirlwind high school activities to pay any heed to the fuss made over him.

But during the time she was traveling between Chicago and Wheaton, freelancing for a daily and editing for a growing Christian magazine, a letter arrived from her mother which *did* get Danni's attention. It was a letter with an article about Logan McGarey's wife of only a few years being killed in a terrible tragedy.

Danni looked up at the man in front of her with sudden compassion. Her journalist's mind recalled most of the details of the article. Logan and his wife had been in Huntsville doing some Christmas shopping. There had been a sniper on the roof of one of the department stores and Logan's wife had been killed. Several other shoppers had been injured that day, too. *How awful it must have been for him ... no wonder he looks so grim and unhappy.*

She realized with a start he'd asked her something. "I'm sorry?"

"Your mother—how is she?"

"Oh—fine! She's just fine, thank you. Did you know my mother?"

He nodded, his expression gentling somewhat. "I used to see her at the service station where I worked part-time after school." He paused for a moment. "She was always very kind—a real nice lady. You look a lot like her."

"Well ... thank you very much." Danni felt strangely awkward with his attempt to be pleasant.

But his tone hardened almost as quickly as it had softened. "Well, ma'am, if you're sure it's what you want to do, I'd suggest you go on out to your house before it gets any later."

Danni noticed that even when he was making a suggestion his voice held a certain edge of command.

He raked his stony gaze over the young people, one at a time. Danni, alert to the curious thread of strain she thought she could detect in his tone, watched his darkened features with interest as he spoke to them.

"You can't do anything about your van before morning," he stated flatly. "And it *is* past curfew, people—you'd best be getting back to the Beetle."

20

"Curfew!" The exclamation tumbled from Danni's mouth before she thought. "Red Oak has a *curfew* now?"

She stepped back instinctively as he fastened a thoughtful stare on her. "I'd imagine, Miss St. John," he said quietly, "that lots of things are different in Red Oak than what you remember. For a number of reasons," he added, with a pointed look at the four Colony members. A muscle flicked at the corner of his mouth, and he touched his now-drenched hair lightly before giving Danni a polite nod.

"Pleasure, ma'am," he murmured, turning his back on all of them to return to the patrol car. But even after he lowered his long frame into the driver's seat, he didn't leave. He simply sat there, waiting until Danni said her good-byes to the young people and drove away from the station.

She wondered what he'd meant, calling the Colony a "Beetle." *Wasn't he a strange one?* she mused as she pulled off Montgomery onto Leander. She turned her windshield wipers on high to fend off the rain which had resumed its earlier assault. There was still no sign of any lights in the houses behind her or ahead of her. She wondered idly how long the sheriff would sit in his patrol car with those disturbing dark eyes of his stalking the young people from the Colony.

How could I have ever thought a cave man like that attractive? she wondered with a wry twist of her mouth. But she quickly answered her own question with the droll reminder that a twelve-year-old girl couldn't be held accountable for her romantic tastes.

It was several minutes later when she noticed the headlights behind her, and she wondered why anyone else would be crazy enough to drive around in a downpour so late at night. But when she turned off Leander onto De Soto and saw that the car was still behind her, closer now, she began to feel a little uneasy. *You're being silly,* Danni told herself sternly. *You are in your hometown—and the most exciting thing that has ever happened in Red Oak was the escape of a somewhat sleepy tiger from a small circus passing through when you were no more than ten.*

Still . . . it *was* awfully dark. And there were no other cars on the street. Just Danni . . . and whoever was following her . . . .

Stop it! There's no one following you! Five hours on rainy country roads has made you a little paranoid, kid—get your act together!

Eighteen-ten De Soto. Even in the darkness, without the benefit of street lights, Danni could tell her home hadn't changed. It was still the same rambling old two-story with the ornate cornices and bannisters. The other children in the neighborhood had often teased her about living in a gingerbread house, but she had never minded. She'd always loved her home. It was big and well-worn and filled with lots of laughter and love and memories.

And now she was back. But her bittersweet thoughts of childhood and all the familiar comforts awaiting her inside were diminished by the anxiety swelling in her throat. That car—the one she'd been so certain wasn't following her—was definitely slowing down, stopping just a few feet down the street. And the driver wasn't getting out. He—or she—was simply sitting there in the darkness in front of the empty corner lot, waiting.

3

Danni gripped the steering wheel, forcing herself to take deep, even breaths. *This is nothing,* she insisted silently. *It's probably just somebody watching for a wandering husband or . . . something. Besides, whatever happened to Danni St. John, fearless girl reporter? Where's the old sense of adventure, kid? We're supposed to be readying our attack on another unsuspecting force of evil and all you can do is sit inside your car and shake in your soggy shoes.*

Slowly and very deliberately, Danni moved her hands away from the steering wheel, zipped her jacket all the way up and squared her shoulders. *I can't sit out here in the driveway all night. I am going to unlock this door, get out, and walk up that driveway and onto the porch. And I'm going to do it right now.*

She removed her keys from the ignition. Her fingers found the house key. Clutching it tightly between her thumb and index finger, she scooped up her leather shoulder bag from the seat and slung it over her arm. With a grim, determined glance out the right hand window, she bit her lower lip and unlocked the car door. Taking one more steadying gulp of air into her lungs, she stepped out. If only there were a light—any kind of light . . . .

Her legs trembled beneath her as she ran up the driveway, keeping watch out of the corner of her eye. The distance to the porch was only a few feet, but it looked endless. A sharp blast of wind and rain blew her hood back from her head, flattening her thick, light hair into a drenched cap about her face.

Danni had almost made it to the bottom step when she

tripped awkwardly over a small branch lying on the walk. She barely avoided a bad fall by grabbing the low-hanging limb of one of the old pin oak trees near the porch. Throwing one last anxious look at the parked car, she took the porch steps two at a time, nearly jerking the storm door off its hinges in her fevered impatience to get inside.

She hadn't realized just how frightened she was until, trying to force the key into the lock, her shaking hands sent the ring clattering noisily onto the porch. Uttering a low groan of frustration, she stooped, glancing furtively out toward the street again before she retrieved the keys and straightened. With her next attempt, she was able to get the key in the lock, but the door wouldn't budge. Hunching her shoulder against the peeling wooden panel, she pushed as hard as she could, but the door held firm.

Her heart thudded to a dead stop when she heard a car door slam. Fingers of icy terror began to inch their way up her back. Still she refused to look anywhere except at her hands on the doorknob. Gripping it with an almost desperate intensity, she heaved her weight against the door one more time. Catlike footsteps approached and Danni willed herself to force down a scream of panic. But when an unexpected circle of bright light framed her against the door, she did scream.

"Need some help?" The voice was soft—and blessedly familiar. The tall, dark sheriff stood at the bottom of the porch steps, training a flashlight on her. There was just enough light for Danni to see an apparent flicker of amusement in his eyes. But she instantly dismissed the thought. Surely nothing would amuse this dour colossus.

Her relief quickly turned to anger when she saw his condescending smile. "I—what are you doing here?" she snapped, irked by the flustered tone of her own voice.

He lowered the beam of the flashlight and took the porch steps slowly and easily, coming to stand directly in front of her. "Just part of the job, ma'am," he said evenly, looking down at her with an expression that now confirmed Danni's suspicion. Without a doubt, the man was enjoying this!

And indeed, Danni had to admit grudgingly to herself, she probably was worth a good laugh or two right now. Her hair was sopping wet and hanging in limp ropes all over her head and what little makeup she wore was long gone, washed away with the last shred of her dignity.

The sheriff was close enough for her to smell the wet leather of his jacket, and she noted with nasty satisfaction that he appeared to be as soaked and miserable as she was.

"Want me to try that?" he asked, looking pointedly from the door to the key ring dangling from her fingers.

"It's stuck," she said unnecessarily, wiping a stream of water from her face with the back of her hand.

His expression was perfectly bland, but Danni still had the feeling that she was the target of his undoubtedly warped sense of humor. "Let me try it," he said brusquely, moving in front of her. He gave the key a quick twist and at the same time leveled a powerful shoulder against the door.

Naturally, it opened with no more than a squeak. Danni looked at his broad back with a mixture of disgust and relief, quickly donning a more polite expression when he turned toward her and motioned her inside. "We'd better see if we can find some candles for you to use tonight," he told her, throwing a path of light in front of her with his flashlight.

"Oh—that's not necessary, really!" she protested, entering the hallway. "I'll be fine now."

An unhealthy odor greeted them as he closed the front door behind him and took her by the arm, keeping the flashlight's beam in front of them. "You'll need candles," he stated matter-of-factly, beginning to move her through the hallway. "An oil lamp would come in handy, too."

Seething inside at his uninvited takeover, Danni refused

to admit to herself that she was grateful he was there. She *did* silently acknowledge the fact that his mood seemed to have improved during the time it had taken him to follow her out here.

"It was you behind me," she mused aloud.

"Hmm?" He flashed the light over the gold and green striped paper on the walls, then started to move Danni toward the living room. "Oh—yeah. Sorry if I scared you. I s'pose I should have identified myself."

"Why did you do it?"

"Do what?"

"Follow me," she said impatiently. "Why did you follow me? It's not exactly a nice night for a drive."

He looked at her as though she were a rare specimen of fungus. When he finally replied, she thought his low voice rumbled a bit more than before.

"It's been a dull night," he said mildly. "I was bored."

When he would have continued to pull her along beside him, Danni stopped short, digging her feet into the one Aubusson carpet in the house and glaring up at him with annoyance. With a look of surprise, he released her arm and waited.

"Are you always this pleasant?" Danni asked with blunt sarcasm.

He studied her, and for just an instant he looked as though he might regret his abrasiveness. But the look quickly disappeared as he turned away from her without a word. He continued to flash the light around the room, a bit too crowded with large, stuffy pieces of Victorian furniture and a wild array of knick-knacks including a fat-globed hurricane lamp. He looked around, and spotting a box of safety matches on the mantel above the fireplace, reached for them to light the wick of the oil lamp.

"Here," he said, handing Danni the flashlight while he held the lamp. "Let's look in the kitchen for some candles."

Somewhat embarrassed now about her shrewishness, Danni stepped in front of him and led the way to the kitchen. "You really don't have to do this," she said grudgingly. "Not that I don't appreciate it, of course."

He didn't answer, but walked into the kitchen and placed the oil lamp in the middle of the big oak, claw-foot table, then began to rummage through drawers beside the outdated double sink.

Danni looked around the room with an unexpected tug of sadness as a whole parade of memories marched through her mind. There had been years and years of evenings spent sitting around that table with her parents. Somehow the kitchen had always been the gathering place for the three of them. Now the comfortable old round table, uncovered and showing its many scars, made the entire kitchen appear sadly empty and strangely unfamiliar.

Lost in her thoughts, she didn't notice the sheriff holding the half dozen or so candles he'd found. "Okay," he said, glancing at her from his place by the counter. "These should do you, even if the power's out until tomorrow."

"What?" She looked at him blankly for a moment, then recovered. "Oh—yes . . . I'm sure they will," she said vaguely. "Thank you, Sheriff," she added, trying to inject a little more warmth into her words. "I really *do* appreciate your helping me like this."

"No problem," he said shortly. "I'll get your luggage out of the car for you and be on my way."

"Oh, really, that's not necessary—"

He held out his hand for the keys he'd returned to her earlier. "Your trunk key?"

Before Danni could protest any further, he took the key ring and his flashlight from her and left the kitchen. She decided his assistance would be a lot easier to take if he didn't seem so . . . so disapproving. She had the uncomfortable feeling that he disliked her for some reason, and, since he'd gone to a lot of trouble for her benefit, she couldn't begin to understand why he found her so offensive.

It occurred to her that it might have something to do with the Colony. She hadn't missed his antagonism toward Brother Penn and the others back at the service station. She shrugged, deciding there was nothing she could do about whatever it was. Picking up the oil lamp, she left the kitchen to take a look at the other rooms on the first floor, heading first toward the den.

The French doors were shut and apparently swollen from the dampness permeating the house. Danni gave the handles a sharp tug, balancing the lamp in her free hand. When they finally creaked open, it was to release an unpleasant, musty odor that made her wrinkle her nose and hold her breath. She hesitated a moment before entering the room that had always been her father's retreat.

Holding the lamp high and extended out in front of her, she took a cautious step forward. Once inside the room, it took her a moment to acclimate herself to the dark shadows that were only faintly relieved by the lamp in her hand.

She saw the broken glass first, shattered in front of the gaping window behind her father's massive mahogany desk. Dazed, she stared at the window for a full minute, feeling the cold wind pouring through the long, narrow opening where glass had been; seeing but not actually registering the fact of the rain blowing in on the soaked, ruined carpet in front of the window.

She had a sickening, oppressive sensation of destruction as she glanced around the room. The drawers had been torn from the desk and thrown aside, their contents spilled in random heaps all over the wet carpet. She was too stunned to make a sound until she looked past the center of the room to the floor-to-ceiling bookshelves and cabinets. The entire collection of her father's books, which her mother had reluctantly left behind because of the limited space in her shared condominium, had been ruthlessly tossed from the shelves and were lying in wet heaps on the floor, most of them obviously beyond saving. In the end, it was the waste, the cruel, meaningless waste of it all that made her scream. And scream again.

The sheriff, just returning from outside, reacted to her scream by throwing the luggage he had tucked under one arm into a heap by the door and hurling himself the rest of the way into the room. Deftly he blocked Danni's small body with his own much larger one. Keeping Danni safely behind his back, he pivoted, his gun ready, his trained gaze expertly assessing the entire room in one sweeping glance. He focused briefly on the broken window, then quickly backed Danni against the wall, still shielding her with his own body.

But the room was empty. Replacing his revolver in its holster, he turned to the small form trembling behind him, grasping both her shoulders with his large, firm hands. "It's all right," he said softly, frowning at Danni's wild-eyed stare.

But it wasn't all right. Danni tried as hard as she could to force the air from her lungs, but she only succeeded in choking. Panic snaked upward through her body, and she felt herself fighting for oxygen as she prayed for just one small breath. Her hands turned into claws as she clutched at the sheriff's shirt front. Her face contorted into raw fear, she somehow managed to mouth one word, "Asthma."

It panicked her even more when she saw his dark, concerned face go stark white. He moistened his lips nervously, and the anxious way his eyes flicked over her told Danni he hadn't a thought of what to do for her. She felt a

29

familiar buzzing in her ears and a charge of nausea hit her mid-section as she realized she was going to lose consciousness any moment.

But the sheriff recovered his wits quickly. Bracing Danni against one arm, he bent to peer into her face. "You got anything with you? In your purse?"

With great effort, Danni nodded, pleading silently with him through large, frightened eyes.

"Your purse? Where's your purse?" He looked around the room, then, without hesitation, scooped her into his arms and raced out into the hallway. Spying her leather bag on the telephone stand at the bottom of the stairs, he lowered himself onto the bottom step and fumbled through her purse. Danni was vaguely aware of the trembling of his hands when he finally pulled the little tube of medication from her purse. She groped for it but her limp hand appeared to be disconnected from her arm, with no feeling or mobility.

"Open your mouth," he ordered harshly. The instant she did, he squeezed the release button to send the liberating medication down her throat into her lungs, watching her closely and drawing in a long, shaky breath of his own when Danni finally gulped in a large swallow of air.

He continued to hold her as her color returned to normal. Weakened by the attack—the worst she'd had in months—Danni lay docilely in his arms, vaguely aware that the man was unexpectedly gentle. He was lightly stroking her still wet hair with the soft, comforting touch of a hand large enough to easily encircle her neck.

Even his voice—a voice she already knew could be alarmingly rough—was low and reassuring as he studied her intently. "Better?"

She nodded weakly. "Thank you." The words were barely audible but deeply sincere.

"D'you go through that often?" Those disturbing dark eyes

30

of his plowed through the defensive self-consciousness associated since childhood with her hated illness.

She shook her head. "Not any more, no. Nothing like it was when I was younger."

"Well," he muttered gruffly, as though he'd suddenly decided he had stepped out of character for long enough, "you get yourself into some dry clothes, if you're able, and I'll take you somewhere else for the night. You can't stay here now."

"What do you mean?" she asked him with a puzzled frown. "Of course, I'm going to stay here!"

"Lady," he growled, abruptly getting to his feet and hauling her up with him, steadying her with his hands on her elbows, "you *did* notice that someone's broken into your house, didn't you?" The scathing look of contempt he settled on her made Danni want to cringe—or slug him.

"I don't have anywhere else to go besides the Colony," she replied with exaggerated patience. "And I can't very well go crawling in there at one o'clock in the morning in the shape I'm in. Not if I want to hold onto the job I just accepted."

Ignoring her defiant glare, he turned her around toward the stairway. "You are *not* spending the night here alone," he grated in the drawl that now did nothing but irritate her. "I have a few other things to do besides sit outside your house in the rain to make sure you stay safe and cozy the rest of the night. You've had an intruder. You have a broken window. You have no lights, and no heat. And you couldn't go out to the Colony even if you wanted to. You wouldn't get in this time of night. They lock the place up tighter than the U.S. Mint after nine o'clock unless you make special arrangements."

Danni laced her tone as thickly as possible with sarcasm. "Well, then, *Sheriff*, just where do you suggest I go?" All too aware that there was no way she could manage anything remotely resembling dignity, standing there miserably wet and exhausted, her knees still shaking under her from the recent bout of wheezing, she nevertheless did her best to stare him down.

For one fleeting moment, Danni thought he was about to smile. A ridiculous notion, of course. He was obviously intent only upon humiliating her.

"Well, now, I know of just the place for you, *Miz* St. John," he answered softly, without a hint of emotion in his tone. "You can spend the night at the County Jail. No charge, of course," he added generously.

4

Three weeks later, seated at her stark white metal desk in the editor's office of the *Peace Standard*, Danni replayed in her mind her first few days back in Red Oak. It would never have occurred to her on that first night back in town that, of all the surprises awaiting her, Sheriff Logan McGarey would turn out to be the biggest one of all. She could even smile now—at least a little—over her night in jail.

The whole experience had been unreal, definitely tops on Danni's list of events she'd never care to repeat. The sheriff had been totally serious that night when he informed her she could use the facilities of the County Jail. Fifteen minutes after she'd hurriedly changed into some dry clothes, he had strong-armed her through the door of the aging, stone County Office Building. He'd then handed her a ragged, disgraceful-looking blanket, and pointed her to a sagging couch in a dark corner of his office.

When she'd ventured a weak complaint about her discomfort some time later, adding the observation that his office was inhumanly cold, he'd glanced up from the file he'd been browsing through, lifted one dark brow and looked at her as though he couldn't remember who she was or what she was doing there. Transferring his gaze back to the papers in front of him, he'd offered her the alternative comfort of one of the cells if she would prefer.

Danni had decided right then and there that she was in the hands of a living prototype of television's exaggerated rednecked lawman.

The next morning he had driven her home, allowing only fifteen minutes to spare before she was supposed to be ready to leave for the Colony. His only attempt at conversation was to ask if he could keep her house keys and look around while she was gone. She'd handed them over grudgingly, instructing him to leave them in the mailbox once he was done.

"You don't want me to do that," he growled. "That's the first place someone looks for a house key. There and over a door frame." He glanced at the garage and motioned to the light above the door. "I'll lay them in the bottom of that light base."

"Fine. So long as you provide a ladder so I can reach them," Danni replied blandly.

He looked at her and Danni was sure he came very close to smiling. "Good point," he said. "How about under that shrub by the garage door?"

She'd been fairly certain that he wouldn't bother her again. The man hadn't exactly kept his contempt a secret. Her last thought of him that morning had contained both relief that the ordeal was over and an annoying drop of regret that he'd been so openly hostile.

But within the next half hour, she'd forgotten about Logan McGarey. The young man called Brother Penn had arrived as promised to guide her out to the Colony. After following the white van out of town and onto an unpaved country road—which she vaguely remembered as the way to the Gunderson farm—Danni drove through a wide, freshly painted open gate. Continuing up a narrow lane that broke through a thick grove of trees, Danni gasped with amazement at the scene which seemed to rise out of the misty woods in front of her. She was so intent on the white, futuristic panorama— unexpectedly stark and out-of-place in this backwoods, rural setting—that she very nearly crashed into the Colony van in front of her.

Her first astonished look at the Colony of the Lotus facilities told her immediately why Logan McGarey had referred to it as the "Beetle." The white, domed building with a number of straight, narrow extensions exploding from the center could, without stretching the imagination too far, be said to resemble an enormous white beetle suspended in the middle of the field.

A closer appraisal revealed two other buildings, also white but much smaller and less impressive, situated behind the main structure. The entire scene was a study in uncluttered, modernistic architecture. The Gunderson farm no longer existed.

If the exterior had left her speechless, the interior absolutely dazed her. Everything—*everything*—was white, including the walls, the plain, cleanly designed furniture, and even the plush carpet. Only the greenery in hanging baskets and an occasional touch of blue in the form of geometric designs on the walls added brief splashes of color. Each Colonist extended the white decor, wearing a simple white toga, unadorned except for a blue sash at the waist and the embroidered blue emblem of the Colony as well as an animal logo on the left shoulder.

Danni had soon learned that the Colonists were divided into ranks, with each rank designated by the name of an animal. The highest rank, which seemed to function as the upper class of the Colony—and the watchdogs of the others, Danni thought—was aptly referred to as the Hawks. These were the only Colonists allowed any freedom whatsoever, as far as she could tell. And it was minimal at best.

Even Reverend Ra, the Master Guide and leader of the Colony, wore a flowing white robe with the same blue pyramid with lotus insert. His, though, had an embroidered scarob beetle over his heart, just barely visible beneath the silver stole he wore about his shoulders. His black, thick-framed eyeglasses were almost owlish, a dramatic contrast to his long silver hair and beard. A tall, commanding man, he would have inspired attention in a business suit, Danni thought, but in the Colony garb he was indisputedly grandiose.

Other than the rather creative philosophy of the Colony, which Danni recognized right away as a blend of Egyptian and Central American Indian mythology, the Colony of the Lotus followed the standard cult format. She didn't pretend to be an expert, but she had spent a number of months researching the cult pattern, and Danni saw no real deviation from it here.

Male and female living quarters were separate, and even the most platonic of relationships between the sexes was apparently discouraged. There was no marriage. They abstained from alcohol, tobacco, sugar and red meat. There was obvious drug abuse, but Danni couldn't tell just how widespread it might be. They emphasized wisdom, enlightenment, simplicity, peace, and love—Colony style. The young people were entirely dependent on Reverend Ra and his assistants for all decisions. Their names were changed as they took on new identities. Their lives centered around their spiritual family. Past ties—family, friends, school—were severed completely. Most of them were young—under twenty—although Danni had seen several elderly men and women on the grounds from time to time.

The students seemed to have no possessions, nor did they display a desire for any. While she hadn't actually been all the way inside any of the living quarters, Danni had managed to sneak a few peeks inside the rooms. They were bleak, decorated in the predictable white motif, and bereft of even the smallest personal items. The only things the Colonists seemed to own consisted of what they needed to maintain personal hygiene.

There was total and unquestioned obedience to Reverend Ra and the Hawks. Danni had already sat in on two faith services, mentally noting the frequent appearance of such phrases as "be disciplined," "control your inner self," "reject the world," "yield to the light of peace," and other meaning-less slogans.

So far, she'd seen nothing she hadn't expected, other than the elderly guests who were rarely observed. They dressed in everyday clothing and seemed to be treated with respect and consideration. But she hadn't been able to come up with any real clue as to what they were doing there.

As overwhelming as she had found the Colony that first day, her response had quickly taken a back seat to the surprise waiting for her when she returned home later that afternoon. She'd found her front door ajar, a glass service truck parked in the driveway, and, despite the chill autumn temperature, every window in the house open! After whirling through a number of rooms and discovering that a major cleanup had apparently taken place throughout, she found Logan McGarey in the library, looking much less intimi-dating in worn jeans and a red sweatshirt as he supervised the installation of a new window.

And he actually *smiled* at her! She was dumbfounded at the change in him when she stammered out some weak, inane question about what he thought he was doing to her house.

"I didn't think you'd mind," he replied offhandedly. "I know Jed Curtis pretty well, and he said you could pay for this whenever you wanted."

When she started to tell him he shouldn't have gone to so much trouble, he simply cut her off with an indifferent, "No problem," and walked across the room to turn on a dehumidifier.

"I figured," he drawled softly, grinning down at her when he returned to the doorway where she was still standing, "you'd be determined to avoid another night in jail—and I thought you might sleep a little better if that window was in."

"But everything has been cleaned up—" Her mind was

37

boggled by his friendliness and the bustle going on around them.

"Not everything," he said. "I just swept up and aired out the rooms. You still have a lot of work to do here."

He hadn't finished surprising her. He went on to apologize for his disposition of the previous night, pleading exhaustion. "I'd been on duty almost forty-eight hours without any sleep," he explained. Then, with a self-mocking smile, he added, "I get a little strange when I don't get my sleep."

"Don't you have any deputies?" she asked him incredulously.

He nodded. "I do, but two of them have the flu, and the other one was at the clinic with his wife all night—they just had a baby a few hours ago. Anyway, I'm sorry if I was a bear. And I'm sure I was."

She was too astonished at the change in him to do more than stutter her understanding. She had tried to pay him for all his work, but that just seemed to irritate him, so she didn't press the issue. However, when she insisted that he be her guest for dinner once she was settled in, he agreed, favoring her with another unsettling smile as he innocently asked if she could cook.

Well, he'd find out soon enough, Danni thought, stirring from her reverie and coming back to the present. He had quickly accepted the invitation she'd offered two days ago and was coming to dinner tonight.

She refused to admit to herself that she was anxious about the evening. She had seen him a number of times since her first week back. Once he had dropped by her house "just to make sure everything was all right." Another time she'd run into him on her way out of the grocery just as he was entering, and they'd had coffee at the deli next door.

But tonight would be different. She denied the word "date" which kept popping into her mind. She suspected Logan McGarey's idea of a date would be much more exciting than a quiet Italian dinner in her kitchen. The thought made her wonder if he'd been interested in anyone since the death of his wife. And then she wondered why she was wondering.

She jumped when Brother Add, the tall, thin, sad-eyed teenager who was her assistant on the *Standard*, interrupted her thoughts by appearing—as he usually did—out of nowhere to stand quietly at her side.

As always, something tugged at her heart when she looked up into his dark eyes. The boy had a loneliness, a "lost" quality about him that made her want to take him under her wing and protect him. He didn't quite fit the mold of the rest of the students. For one thing, he seemed more alert most of the time, more interested in little things. And he was highly creative, Danni had discovered. His talents extended from the technical aspects of the printing process to sketching and layout.

"Hi, Add. Classes over?"

"Yes, Sister—Miss St. John," he stammered softly.

Like most of the other students she'd met, Add seemed to have a problem with her insistence on being called by her given name, rather than the Sister or Brother used by everyone else at the Colony. She had explained to Add that she was merely an employee, not a member, and encouraged him to simply call her Danni. So far, however, he couldn't seem to manage that.

"Reverend Ra wants to see you," he told her now. "He said I should ask if you'd come to his office, please." The boy spoke softly and hesitantly, as though he wasn't sure he should be speaking at all.

She sighed, but only to herself as she got up from her desk. She started to leave the office but abruptly changed her mind and returned for her raincoat. The *Standard's* offices and printing facilities were in one of the smaller, detached buildings in back of the main structure. It was only a few feet away, but the cold rain that had come and gone during the first week of Danni's return home had unleashed itself on them again, and she had learned the hard way, because of her asthmatic condition, to avoid colds.

Standing at the doorway of Reverend Ra's office, Danni hesitated a moment before knocking, purposely delaying her entrance. She hadn't been surprised when she found herself disliking the large, florid faced man. She'd known when she researched the job she wouldn't like him; that was to be expected. But what she hadn't anticipated was the way he made her feel about nine years old, dimwitted, and slightly threatened.

Few people intimidated Danni. With the work she had done for the past few years—and her natural, honest assumption that she was directly under the Lord's protection—she simply went where she had to go and did what she felt she had to do.

But this man was an exception. In spite of his whitewashed, saintly manner, and his long, flowing robes and ever-present smile, Danni had sensed some elusive aura of contamination about him right from the beginning. He made her uncomfortable and he made her angry. And, even though she routinely attempted to deny it, he made her afraid.

Although he had called out his permission for her to enter when she knocked, she found him in his meditation posture when she walked in. As soon as she saw him standing in front of the wall-to-wall glass window, his arms extended straight out in front of him, his eyes closed as he mouthed some sort of chant, Danni started to turn and leave. But he motioned her with one hand to stay, opening his eyes and smiling kindly at her.

"Sister . . . come in, come in. I thought we'd have a nice chat before you leave for the weekend. Sit down, please." He walked over to his white desk—Danni thought he seemed more to *ooze* than to walk—and seated himself, gesturing for her to take the chair directly across from him.

"I've been wanting to tell you how pleased I am with what you've accomplished so far," he stated, smiling broadly as she sat down. "I'm already convinced you have the ability to make the *Standard* the effective vehicle for this community which I've long envisioned."

Uncertain as to how she was expected to reply to his praise, Danni managed only a quiet, "Thank you." Reluctantly keeping her gaze level with his, she felt again the sick, cold feeling those pale blue eyes never failed to generate.

"I must admit," he went on with a chuckle, "that some of my assistants here questioned my judgment in hiring a rather unknown journalist I'd never even met." His gaze sharpened to a piercing stare, and Danni had to force herself not to look away when she replied.

"I . . . wondered about that myself—Reverend Ra." She made an effort not to choke on the title.

He shrugged, raising both hands palm upward. "Your portfolio was simply too impressive to ignore, my dear. For one so young, you have accomplished much. I felt led to trust you." He gave his last few words careful emphasis. "Besides, it's rather . . . difficult . . . to find a competent person who wants to take up residence in a rural area like this. Of course," he continued smoothly, "with it being your home, it's only natural you'd want to return. Although I confess to being somewhat surprised, since your mother no longer lives here."

"That's true," Danni said quickly, "but I promised myself years ago that one day I'd come back to Red Oak to settle. I'm a Dixie girl at heart, I'm afraid."

"Well, that's certainly to our advantage, Sister." His syrupy voice rankled Danni, but she had to admit that the man *did* have a way about him. He might be as phony as a nine-dollar bill, but he somehow managed to exude a deceptive sincerity that engendered a dangerous amount of trust on

41

the part of his followers. She'd already seen for herself that he was adored—indeed, *worshipped*—by the Colonists. For her part, Danni wouldn't have trusted him with last week's weather report.

"I expect," he continued in a less sugary tone, "truly great things from you and the *Standard* in the future, Sister. We hope to move from our present weekly format into a daily soon, as I explained to you when you were hired. Naturally, I'll be most interested in your progress in that direction."

Danni glanced at him sharply. Why did his words make her feel as though she were being warned? "I appreciate your faith in me, sir." She got to her feet, desiring to end this conversation as quickly as possible. "I do need to finish up some things before I leave. Will that be all?"

He rose from his chair, extending his right hand to her, just as he always did at the end of one of these interviews. "Yes, you must be tired from the long hours you've been putting in this week. I'm sure you're looking forward to getting some rest over the weekend."

"Yes—yes, I am," she agreed. Anxious to leave the office, she offered a firm handshake and quickly left.

As she hurried back to her office and began closing up for the day, she found herself thinking—and was greatly surprised when she realized the direction her thoughts had taken—that what she was looking forward to wasn't rest at all. Instead, she found herself anticipating the inexplicably safe, comfortable feelings that accompanied the image of Sheriff Logan McGarey. As a matter of fact, the way she felt around him was a striking contrast to the uneasiness she experienced in the presence of Reverend Ra.

Without really understanding why, she felt a strong desire for the shelter the black-bearded law officer suddenly represented.

5

Exactly fifteen minutes before the sheriff was due to arrive, Danni was downstairs in the living room waiting. She had dressed up more than she usually would have. She wore a black silk Indian-print pullover dress with a fringed skirt, and had coaxed soft waves into her mid-length hair. In spite of her determination that this was not a date, the truth was that Logan McGarey was an extremely attractive, intriguing man. And, although he continued to puzzle her and even exasperate her, she was excited about the evening ahead.

The doorbell shattered her thoughts. He was early, too, and Danni wondered fleetingly if that meant he was looking forward to being with her. She took a deep, steadying breath before opening the door.

She was immediately thrown off-center by two things: The unexpected flicker of pleasure in his eyes when he saw her, and the obvious effort he'd made to look nice. Danni reacted to both in spite of herself.

She made a real effort to appear composed, but unconsciously fingered the silky material at her collarbone. He stood there, smiling awkwardly, and Danni noticed how much younger he looked tonight. His black hair was neatly trimmed, as was his beard. A light blue crewneck sweater showed beneath his darker blue flight jacket. In his left hand, he clutched a lovely but unpretentious bouquet of fall flowers.

He handed her the bouquet as he stepped inside. "If this is corny, I apologize," he said dryly. "I may be a little rusty in the social department."

Surprised by his words, Danni stared at the flowers for a

moment, then recovered. "Some things never go out of style, Sheriff," she assured him with a smile. "They're lovely—thank you."

"You know," he drawled slowly while shrugging out of his jacket and draping it over the small desk chair in the hallway, "I *am* off-duty tonight. My name's Logan."

"Oh—of course," Danni stammered. "Please, come in. I'm going to get these into water right away."

He followed her through the dining room into the kitchen. "I hope you don't mind—one of my deputies will be dropping off some papers here later. I wanted to take them out to the farm with me tonight to read, but they weren't ready earlier. Is that all right?"

"Of course," Danni said, lifting the lid on a large pan to peek inside.

"Ah—do I smell Italian?"

"Yes. Do you like it? I'm afraid I don't have many specialties in the kitchen, and most people seem to like spaghetti—" She knew she was chattering and wondered irritably what there was about this man that made her feel so ridiculously young and awkward.

"And just what are your specialties, Danni St. John?" Logan asked as he straddled a chair backwards.

"What? Oh . . . . " She laughed lightly and shrugged. "I'm afraid about the only place I can hold my own is in front of a word processor—or a typewriter."

Nodding agreeably, he motioned to the salad Danni had begun to toss. "Want me to do that?" he asked.

"Well . . . if you don't mind. I can get the bread ready, then."

Danni was surprised at the effortless way he made himself at home in her kitchen, helping himself to utensils and then loading the dishwasher after he'd tossed the salad. She learned quite a lot about him in those few minutes before dinner, and even more during the meal. The contrasts in the man were fascinating.

She discovered that he lived on a small farm; had an Irish setter named Sassy; enjoyed a wide variety of music—including bluegrass and gospel; was "near addicted" to buttermilk; and had a black belt in karate. He was also well educated with a master's degree in forensic science and a specialty in toxicology. She wondered why he'd chosen to stay in a town the size of Red Oak.

Logan was also an expert at interviewing. Before they were through their meal, Danni had revealed her weakness for chocolate cake, french fries doused in vinegar, and banana ice cream topped with roasted peanuts. She admitted to a total ineptitude with appliances, an old aversion for instruction books, and a new fondness for Vivaldi. She even confided to him that she had always been hopelessly and helplessly absentminded.

She found herself laughing easily at his unexpectedly sharp sense of humor and warming to his pleasant, casual manner. They ate their meal accompanied by companionable chatter. Logan voiced an occasional compliment about the food and Danni asked questions about what had been happening in Red Oak during her absence.

He offered to get a fire going in the living room while she made coffee. He was on his second cup of what he referred to as "coffee with character" when he spied the gray Victorian dollhouse resting on a table by the doorway.

He walked over to examine it, tracing the line of its mansard roof with his index finger. Dipping his head, he studied the miniature furnishings set in perfect place inside. It was excellently crafted with intricate detail.

"This is really nice," he said admiringly. "I always thought that if I ever had a little girl, I'd want her to have one of these."

Surprised at the almost wistful note in his voice, Danni went to stand by him. "You . . . don't have any children?"

45

He glanced at her, then looked away. "No. But you know I was married . . . . " He returned his gaze to her, and Danni was touched by the mixture of resignation and sadness in his eyes.

She nodded. "Yes." Hesitating uncertainly, she added, "I'm sorry, Logan . . . about your wife."

He didn't look away from her, but spoke slowly and thoughtfully. "You wouldn't have known Teresa. She was from Dallas." He bent down again to peer inside the dollhouse. "We met when I was in school there. We were married right after I got my first duty as a street cop."

When he straightened, his eyes met hers and he smiled softly, as though to tell her it was all right that they were speaking of his wife. "You would have liked her," he said easily. "She was . . . special."

Abruptly, he shook off the melancholy edging his mood. "Was this yours, when you were a little girl?" he asked, gesturing to the dollhouse.

"No, it's not that old."

He looked at her curiously, then grinned. "Ah—I know. You're still a little girl at heart, and this is your hobby."

"In a way," Danni agreed, smiling at him. "I built it."

He glanced from her to the dollhouse. "Really?"

Danni nodded. "My father used to make them. It was a pastime of his, and he taught me how. I've built a dozen or so for relatives and friends. This is one of mine," she said. "But I have one in my bedroom my dad made. It's a Georgian style, much larger than this one. He won a prize for it one year at the state fair."

Logan's eyes went over her face slowly, studying the tousled light hair, the oval face, the dark brown doe eyes, the pert, slightly upturned nose where a few scattered freckles bounced. A flicker of something akin to amusement—but much warmer—leaped in his gaze, then faded.

"You're a lady of surprises, Danni St. John," he said softly.

46

He moved away, walking over to the fireplace where he dropped down to a large, worn hearth cushion in front of the fire. Danni made herself comfortable on the couch, curling up at one end with her feet tucked under her. Her silk dress whispered each time she moved to retrieve her coffee cup from the floor in front of her.

Resting his arms on his propped up knees, staring thoughtfully into the fire, Logan spoke without looking at her. "Why did you come back here, Danni? Why did you take the job at the Colony?"

Danni hesitated. He was a man accustomed to getting answers to his questions, she knew, and the question was a natural one. Any evasion on her part could easily make him suspicious.

"Well . . . it was a chance to come home," she began. He turned toward her, intently watching her face. Hearing the slight waver in her voice, she cleared her throat and tried for a firmer tone. "And I've always wanted to edit a local paper. It's a wonderful opportunity to learn management as well as marketing. Being a reporter is fun, but the leg work gets old after a while."

Logan nodded agreeably as though he understood. "I'm sure it does. But I'm a little puzzled about something. I remember your parents as committed Christian people." His eyes narrowed slightly as he measured her reaction. "Doesn't it bother your mother, your working for a . . . *cult?*"

Frustration stabbed at Danni. She knew what it looked like to Logan, and every time she was with him she flinched at his disapproval of what she was doing. But she couldn't tell him the truth, not yet. She'd learned in the past to cut her risks as much as possible by working alone and keeping her mouth shut. This might well be the most dangerous set of circumstances in which she'd ever been involved. Her silence at this point was essential. Once she had the story, then, if she and Logan were still . . . friends . . . she could tell him what it had all been about. But not now. For now, she'd simply have to allow him to think the worst: That she had sold out, for whatever reasons.

She chose her words very carefully, deliberately looking at the blazing fire instead of meeting his gaze. "I'm a Christian, too, Logan. And I suppose it does seem strange to some people, but it's just a job, after all. I don't have to accept their philosophy to edit the newspaper."

She looked at him then, wanting to shrink from what she saw in his eyes, the disillusionment—and what appeared to be a touch of anger as well.

"*Philosophy?* Is that what you call what goes on out there?"

It was impossible to ignore the disgust in his voice. Danni steeled herself and went on the offensive.

"And just exactly what *does* go on out there?"

The glint in his eyes became steely. "I'm not sure—at least not yet." He stood up, stretching his long, rangy form. "But I can tell you this—the place is rotten. They may enforce any number of rules about healthy eating and clean living and peace and love and the *family*," he rasped contemptuously, "but they're a bunch of crooks without a conscience and the only *philosophy* they adhere to is greed."

Surprised at the vehemence of his tone, Danni countered, "How do you know all this?"

He rested an elbow on the mantel and stood quietly, staring at her. "I can't prove it. Right now all I've got is a bunch of aggravating bits and pieces that don't add up the way I want them to. But I've got enough to know they're dangerous people. Too rough for a pretty young girl to get herself involved with. Why don't you try the *County Herald?* They'd probably put you on, if you just want a job here in Red Oak."

She'd already anticipated that someone might eventually suggest this very thing. "Logan, the *County Herald* already has an editor. And," she added quickly, "an assistant editor."

He lifted his brows and shrugged. "What about Scotts-boro? It's not that far away from home. Why did you want to come back here, anyway? Your mother's gone. Do you have other family here?"

Danni shook her head. "No. No family." She thought about his question for a moment and realized that, at least in part, her answer would be the truth. "I love this town. I love Alabama. I always knew I'd come back some day." She gave him a small, tight smile. "Why do *you* stay here? With your education and experience, you could get a job with any law enforcement agency in the country."

He shrugged, returning her smile. "I s'pose my reason's pretty much the same as yours. It's home. I don't really want to live anywhere else. Of course," he said with a light chuckle, "if I don't get re-elected, I may have to research the assets of another area."

"Is that a possibility?" Danni asked, surprised at how much the thought upset her.

He finished the last drop of coffee in his cup before he answered. "With a political job, that's *always* a possibility. The guy who's running against me next year has a pretty impressive slate."

"Who is he?"

"Carey Hilliard. He's an attorney. Set up practice in town about two years ago. He's chaired quite a few important committees and, so I've been told, has a very impressive list of influential friends."

"Are you worried?"

He shrugged again. "He makes me a little uneasy, I guess. He just seemed to appear out of nowhere. The next thing I know, he's a real VIP."

Danni's next statement was as much a surprise to her as it might have been to Logan. "If I can help you, I'd be glad to." When he inclined his head with a questioning look, she explained. "I helped pay my college expenses by writing campaign speeches and drafting resumes."

He looked pleased—and interested—for a moment, but his expression sobered abruptly. "You might want to reconsider your offer. Hilliard is a real fair-haired boy with the Reverend Ra."

Stung by what he was implying, Danni's eyes sparked with anger. "I work for the Colony, Logan. But that's all. They don't own me."

His gaze burned through her as he narrowed his eyes and studied her face. "Sooner or later, Danni," he said softly, "they own anyone who gets involved with them. Be careful."

He moved his arm away from the mantel and walked toward her. "Let's change the subject, okay? I've been wanting to talk to you about something else." He sat down beside her on the couch. He was close enough that they could have touched, and Danni felt slightly overwhelmed, as she had before, by his formidable size and obvious strength.

"Can you think of any reason for someone to break into your house? Anything special they might be looking for?"

Danni frowned in confusion. "A reason? No, there's nothing here that anyone would be interested in." She looked at him closely. "Why?"

He raked his fingers through his hair, then rested his arm on the back of the couch. "I found something the day I searched the house. It may be nothing, but it bothers me."

"What?" Danni was instantly alert.

"I found a scrapbook, in the den. It had a lot of stuff about you in it—looked like something your folks might have kept."

Danni smiled, immediately aware of what he was talking about. "Yes. My mother's kept a scrapbook of me for years—

ever since junior high, I think."

"Nothing wrong with that," Logan said with a small smile. "But what I'm wondering about . . . it looked as though some things might be missing from it."

"Missing?" Danni stared at him, puzzled.

He nodded. "On the last couple of pages, it looks as though some clippings have been taken—pulled loose from the tape. Do you have any idea what might have been on those pages?"

Danni shook her head in bewilderment. "Nothing important. Probably just stuff about college—or maybe my book on abortion clinics. Is the scrapbook still in the den?"

"In the bottom desk drawer. With a couple of photo albums. Why did your mother leave it here instead of taking it with her when she moved to Florida?"

Danni shrugged. "She left a lot of personal things like that. She said she wanted me to have them, now that I'm older." Rising from the couch, she walked over to the mantel and picked up his empty coffee cup. "Why don't you get the scrapbook while I make some more coffee? Maybe I'll be able to figure out what's missing."

Within moments, he joined her in the kitchen. Opening the scrapbook to the section he'd told her about, he scooted a chair up beside her.

"Well, you're right," Danni said quietly, her voice troubled as she stared at the pages. "Something's obviously been removed. But I can't think of a single reason for anyone taking something out of here. Do you think this has anything to do with the house being vandalized?"

"I think that's a definite possibility, yes. You don't have any idea what it could be?" he asked, gesturing to the open scrapbook in front of them.

"None. It could have been anything. I'm afraid my mother has a tendency to clip every little article or picture that's even remotely related to my career."

She set her cup down and turned to find Logan staring thoughtfully at her. His face was very close to hers, and for one fleeting second she completely lost her train of thought.

"You were blessed with a very special family, weren't you?" he asked softly.

"Why—yes. Yes, I suppose I was," she stammered, surprised and flustered as she searched his eyes to identify the emotion she had heard in his voice. But whatever had prompted his question was already gone, leaving only a warm flicker of interest in his midnight eyes.

They both jumped, startled, when the doorbell shrilled. "That's probably Phil," Logan said, rising from his chair. Danni followed him out of the kitchen and down the hallway to answer the door.

A fairly tall, decidedly handsome man in a tan uniform greeted them with a lazy smile and an assessing stare at Danni. His charcoal gray eyes darted an amused glance from her to Logan, standing behind her.

"Ma'am—sorry to bother you, but I need to see the sheriff."

"Yes, come in." Danni turned to Logan, who moved slightly closer.

"Danni, this is Philip Rider, one of my deputies. Philip, Danni St. John."

Removing his uniform hat, the deputy acknowledged the introduction. "Pleasure, ma'am." He allowed his bold gaze to linger on Danni's face an uncomfortably long time before returning his attention to the much taller man standing beside her.

Danni noticed the warmth in Logan's gaze as he looked at the younger man, but she felt oddly disturbed by what appeared to be a hint of—contempt?—in the deputy's attitude toward Logan. She decided quickly that she must be imagining things because Rider's tone, when he spoke, was polite and respectful.

"Sorry to interrupt, Logan, but you said to drop this off."

Logan nodded, taking the thin manila file folder from the deputy. "What about tonight? You checked out the bus station?"

"Right. But no one came in. And no one from the Colony was there, either," he added, glancing quickly at Danni.

"Mmm. Well, thanks for bringing this to me, Phil. Everything's quiet?"

"Oh, yeah. The usual Friday night stuff. Nothing heavy." He turned to Danni once more. "Well, I'd better get going. It was real nice meeting you, Miss St. John. Hope to see you again soon."

Danni shut the door behind him and turned to find Logan pulling on his jacket. "It's late," he said. "You'd probably like to get some rest."

She walked with him to the door. When he looked down at her, his gaze clouded with concern. "Danni," he said soberly, a slight frown creasing his forehead, "you'll be careful when you're out there—at the Colony?"

Danni felt a rush of dizzying pleasure at the warmth in his words. The idea that he cared about her welfare pleased her more than it should have. "Yes, of course I will."

He nodded, and for a moment seemed about to say something else. Raising one large hand as if to touch her cheek, he hesitated, then dropped his arm back to his side. "Thanks for dinner. You make great spaghetti." Again, he hesitated. "I'd like to call you tomorrow?"

It was a definite question, and Danni responded quickly. "I'll be here. I'm just going to clean house a bit and do some reading."

And then he was gone, leaving her to wonder at her unexpected, disturbing attraction to this enigmatic man.

Within a few brief hours, her professionally honed senses had identified Logan McGarey as a complex, unpredictable man—a gentle man of strength, a restless, somewhat unhappy man, and a rather intimidating man who yet possessed a rare compassion.

Uneasily, Danni summed up her feelings about the evening by reluctantly admitting it had only served to pique her interest in the big, puzzling sheriff whose absence left the room strangely empty and cold.

6

Danni had almost forgotten how her home state could produce a deceptively warm, gentle day even in November to tease the hardest of hearts with a subtle touch of springtime. This had been one of those days, and by late afternoon she was restless, enticed into daydreaming by the warm sweetness of the day. And her daydreams, in spite of all her efforts to thwart their direction, had continually focused on Logan McGarey.

She hadn't seen him for over a week, since the night they had had dinner together at her house. He had called her the next day, but hadn't attempted to see her. And she was hurt. Worse, she was angry—not at Logan, but at herself for allowing the man to gain such a foothold on her emotions so quickly.

Danni knew she was surprisingly inexperienced when it came to romance. Actually, there had been no time for her to form any lasting relationships. Aside from one or two high school boyfriends, she had purposely kept herself uncommitted. Working part-time to help pay her college expenses, then maintaining a frantic career pace over the last few years, she had avoided any kind of relationship that held so much as a hint of potential seriousness. And to date, she hadn't met anyone to change her mind.

So her attraction to the somewhat exasperating sheriff was not only puzzling to her but slightly annoying as well. She simply didn't need any complications in her life right now, especially one like Logan McGarey. She had a job to do, a job that demanded one hundred percent concentration on her part. But the harder she tried not to think about him, the more he insinuated himself into her thoughts. And the harder it became to erase his dark, stern features—which could turn gentle when she least expected it—from her mind.

It wasn't as if she didn't have enough to think about. So far she'd found nothing in the way of surprises at the Colony. She had taken a few pictures with her mini-cam of the grounds and sneaked a couple of inside shots during the last faith service. But there was nothing that would even raise eyebrows. She knew the story was here. How to unravel it was another matter.

Two things happened later that afternoon to contribute to her restlessness and spur her frustration. Both occurred within the same hour, and both involved men.

She felt strangely disappointed when she lifted the telephone receiver in answer to its strident ring and heard the low, smooth drawl of Philip Rider, Logan's deputy.

"Miss St. John—Danni? Hi, this is Phil Rider. Remember me?"

Surprised, Danni answered politely, "Yes, of course. How are you?"

"Just fine, thanks. I was wondering if you'd have dinner with me tonight?"

She stared wordlessly at the phone for a moment, not understanding her reluctance to accept. The young deputy was handsome to the point of distraction and hopefully single, since he was asking for a date. She should have been flattered and eager to accept his invitation. Instead, she found herself grateful she had a valid excuse to turn him down.

"Oh—well, that's awfully nice of you, but I'm afraid I can't tonight—"

"Tomorrow then?" he persisted. "I'm off until Saturday."

"I—" Why in the world was she saying no? "I'm terribly sorry, but I can't."

He sounded sincerely disappointed. "I hope you won't mind if I try again—unless, of course, that cousin of mine has you sewed up already."

"Cousin?"

"Logan." His tone was light, but Danni thought she detected a slight edge to it. "I'll have to remind him that rank isn't supposed to apply when we're off duty."

"What?" Danni stammered blankly. "I didn't realize you were related."

"Well, Logan's always been more like a big brother to me than a cousin. Listen, I won't keep you. But I *will* call you again—if it's all right?"

"Oh . . . yes. Of course."

Glancing up to discern the shadow that had just fallen across her desk, she encountered her second surprise of the day. Logan McGarey was standing in the doorway of her office. His dark hair was slightly ruffled and his wire-framed, aviator sunglasses rested on the rather prominent bridge of his nose. He was in shirtsleeves and appeared mildly amused at Danni's flustered reaction to his presence.

Startled, and entirely too pleased by his appearance, Danni wondered how much of her conversation with his cousin he might have overheard. "Well—hello!" she said weakly.

He removed his sunglasses, hooking them over the edge of his shirt pocket. "Busy?"

"Not really. I should be, but it's hard to concentrate on a day like this."

"It's a dandy," he agreed, walking the rest of the way into her office. "How've you been?"

They made meaningless small talk for a few seconds before he finally sat down in a chair across from her desk. "I just had a nice chat with your boss. Smooth, isn't he?" His smile was still in place, but Danni thought his eyes glinted with a spark of something unpleasant.

"What do you mean?"

He shrugged, his dark brows lifting in a sardonic expression. "Let's just say that the . . . *Master Guide* is also a master of evasion."

"Evasion?" Danni repeated. "I don't understand."

With a level gaze, he assessed her reaction. "How much contact do you have with him? Does he keep pretty close tabs on your job?"

Danni flipped the switch on her word processor to turn it off, then leaned forward, resting both elbows on the desktop. Lacing her fingers together, she propped her chin on them, studying the sheriff with curiosity.

She acknowledged his question with one of her own. "Why do you dislike him so much?"

He looked away from her. "Cop instincts, maybe? I don't know." Returning his gaze to her, he disarmed her with a smile.

"So—whose heart were you breakin' when I came in?" His tone was teasing as he nodded to the telephone.

Danni felt her face grow warm, wondering again how much he'd heard. "Your, uh, cousin, as a matter of fact," she stammered.

"Philip?" His smile remained in place, but Danni thought his voice was a little strained. "Well, now, that boy doesn't get turned down too often. He may never be right again."

She laughed lightly. "Popular, is he?"

"You might say that," Logan replied agreeably. "So he told you we're family?"

"Yes. I get the impression he's about to accuse you of pulling rank on him, too."

He grinned. "Only if I have to. I heard you say you're busy tonight." He hesitated an instant, then continued. "I was hoping you might take a drive with me over to Scottsboro. I have to pick up some papers, and I thought maybe we could have dinner on the way back. This is the first free evening

I've had all week."

Danni was sharply disappointed, then troubled by the sense of relief she felt when she realized that his reason for not calling had been his job. "Oh, Logan—I'd really like to! But I'm working until at least ten tonight."

He frowned. "Why so late?"

She hesitated, reluctant to discuss any part of her job with him, knowing it would just incur his displeasure. "We're doing a special edition tomorrow and I'm snowed under."

He crossed his arms over his chest. "Special edition?" he asked casually. "For what?"

"Oh, it's an anniversary issue. You know—'Highlights of the Last Five Years'—that type of thing."

She almost cringed at the scorn that settled over his features. "Right." He was quiet for a long moment, staring at the floral paperweight on her desk. "The *Standard's* circulation is unusually high, you know. That's kind of strange, isn't it? For a private weekly newspaper?"

Danni shrugged. "It happens. It *is* a good paper, Logan. And I'm not saying that simply because I'm the editor. Someone had already done an excellent job with it long before I was hired."

"Oh, I don't deny that. But most cults—don't frown at me, Danni, this *is* a cult, whether you like the word or not—most cults don't make any effort to branch out into the community. Just the opposite. Almost without exception, they stay totally isolated except for what money they can milk from people on the outside."

He leaned forward on his chair. "A few of them publish in-house newsletters, but they're ordinarily focused entirely on the organization. Nothing like what the Lotus is doing. They're actually competing with the *County Herald.*"

"It's true they intend to increase their coverage," Danni admitted. "I was hired with the understanding that I'd expand circulation and broaden the overall influence of the

59

paper. What's wrong with that?"

"Maybe nothing," he replied with a small shrug. "But I can't help being a little curious as to what they're up to. Frankly, I've got a hunch they're after political clout, and the power that goes with it."

"And that bothers you?"

He leaned back in the white, plastic-covered chair that was almost too small for him. When he finally answered, he spoke quietly and evenly. "There's very little about the Colony of the Lotus," he said, "that doesn't bother me. Very little."

"Well," Danni said with a shaky laugh, "I guess I know where that leaves me."

"Oh, I doubt that," he said softly, pushing himself up from the chair. "You're not going to work in here alone tonight, are you?"

Danni looked up at him, wondering what he was getting at. "No. Add will be here with me."

"Add?"

"My assistant. Add is his Colony name."

Logan nodded. "Is he conscious most of the time?"

"What is *that* supposed to mean?" Danni asked sharply.

"Well, in case you haven't noticed," he drawled, "most of the students around here are a little fuzzy-headed."

She had noticed, of course, but didn't want to alert him just yet as to how much she knew. "I don't think that's fair. You have to remember that the people in this place are studying or—well, what they call *meditating* most of the time. They're very placid, very unemotional."

"Very stoned," he added dryly.

He had merely given voice to what she already knew. "Stoned?"

"Unless you are extremely naive—and I somehow don't think you are—you know exactly what the word means," he challenged. Without warning, he then changed the subject.

60

"Isn't there a lunch room or a lounge over in the main building?"

"There's a cafeteria, yes. Why?"

"Are you allowed a break?"

"Yes."

"Fine. Buy me a cup of coffee." Then, grinning as though he enjoyed goading her, he added, "Or do they make coffee here? Will I have to settle for turnip tea or something?"

Danni stood up, scowling nastily at him. "You can be a very difficult man, do you know that?"

Still grinning, he took her by the arm as she came around the desk. "That's one of the nicer things I've heard about myself, Miz St. John. You flatter me."

"Probably," she agreed.

As she sat across from him at a table in the starkly white, spotlessly clean cafeteria, she noted again his dark skin with its unusual bronze cast, and the high cheekbones that appeared to have been sculpted. Never known for her tact, she asked abruptly, "Do you, by any chance, have an American Indian in your ancestry?"

A twinkle came into his eyes as he lifted his brows. "It shows, huh?"

"I knew it," Danni said, pleased with herself.

"My grandmother was Cherokee," he said. " 'Course, there's a story that's been passed down over the years that she was also a descendant of Tascalusa."

Danni pondered the name, trying to remember her history. "Tascalusa . . . that rings a bell . . . . "

"His name meant *Black Warrior*. He was the Indian chief De Soto defeated at the battle of Mabila. Supposedly, he had black hair, black eyes, stood over seven feet tall and was mean—real mean."

Danni's mouth quirked. "Could be some truth to that family legend, you know. Makes a lot of sense, if you think about it."

"Oh, I've never doubted it," he agreed, taking a deep sip of coffee. "So," he said lightly, changing the subject, "you think I'm wrong about the drugs? You don't think that the kids seem a little vacant most of the time?"

Danni glanced uneasily about the room, but it was empty except for her and Logan. "I'm really not around the students that much. I spend most of my day in the *Standard* offices," she explained. "About the only time I see anyone besides Add or Reverend Ra is at noon when I come in here for lunch. Or when I take a walk around the grounds in the afternoon."

"Well, I don't pretend to be an expert on many things," he said slowly, staring down at his coffee cup, "but I do know when a kid's mind is being messed with. And I feel reasonably sure you've got a bunch of teenagers out here whose brains are being turned to mush." When he glanced up at her, the lines of his face were hard and his eyes even darker than usual. "And I'm not sure that's all."

"What do you mean?"

"I don't know, Danni," he admitted, sighing heavily. "Right now it's still a hunch." He surprised her by reaching over and touching her hand. "Just . . . be careful, okay?"

Pleased by his obvious concern, Danni swallowed with difficulty and nodded. "You said you were here to talk with Reverend Ra?"

"Mm-hmm. Routine stuff. I have to try to locate any family of an old man who died a few weeks ago, while he was . . . visiting here."

Danni remembered hearing the death notice on the radio that first night she arrived in town. "So—did you learn anything?"

His gaze flicked over her face. "No. But I didn't expect to. It was the same with the other two."

Danni couldn't halt the startled exclamation that escaped her. "*Other* two!"

He nodded, tracing the rim of his cup with his index finger. "William Kendrick died, supposedly of a heart attack, while he was staying at the Colony. He was the third visitor to have a heart attack within five months. Something about that doesn't set right with me."

When Danni said nothing, Logan continued. "All three were apparently indigent. No surviving family members could be located for any of them. None of them had so much as a charge card or a driver's license on them. The first man was found in the woods back of the Colony. They said he was senile and had wandered off in the night.

"About six weeks later, another elderly man was found dead in his bed in the guest quarters. And then Kendrick died a few weeks ago while he was taking a walk one afternoon. Just fell over, apparently."

"But weren't the deaths investigated? A coroner—"

Logan frowned impatiently. "I did the best I could. Ed Johnson, the county coroner, examined all three of them. But we weren't able to get releases to do autopsies, so his hands were virtually tied. It looked as though each of them died of a heart attack, but—" He shook his head doubtfully and rubbed a hand over the back of his neck.

"But you're not comfortable with that."

"Would you be?" he countered sharply. "Doesn't the . . . *coincidence* bother you a little?"

She nodded slowly. "What do you think it means?"

He started to reply, then seemed to think better of it. Silence hung between them for several moments before Danni broke it. Glancing at her watch, she rose from her chair, saying, "I suppose I should get back."

Logan nodded, rising from his chair. He stood unmoving for a long moment, looking down at her and searching her eyes as though he were measuring her possible reaction to something. Then, seeming to settle a question within himself, he spoke quietly. "When can I see you again?"

"Oh—well, I—" Danni was surprised, by the question, his directness, and her pleasure.

"You're working tonight, I'm working tomorrow night. That takes us up to Sunday."

"It does, doesn't it?" She thought for a moment. "Well, we could go to church—and then have lunch?"

He glanced away. "I don't think so."

Danni looked at him in surprise. When he made no attempt to explain, the natural directness which made skirting an issue next to impossible for her, took over. "Don't you go to church?"

The small muscle at his right eye twitched slightly. "Not lately, I haven't, no."

"But you used to. You used to go to the same church I did. I remember—"

He couldn't seem to stop a smile at her bluntness. "Is this an interview, or off the record?"

She had the grace to blush. "Sorry. Occupational hazard. I didn't mean to pry."

"But?" He waited.

"I . . . just wondered why, that's all."

He shrugged evasively. "I'm not sure myself anymore."

"I'm sorry," Danni said quickly. "It's really none of my business."

He looked relieved. "What about you?" His voice thickened with sarcasm. "Doesn't the Reverend object to your going to church somewhere else rather than here at the Colony?"

She lifted her chin. "No one," she stated with emphasis, "tells me where to go to church."

He reached into his shirt pocket for gum, offering a stick to Danni, which she refused. "Somehow that doesn't surprise me," he said slowly with an affectionate grin. "As a matter of fact," he added, "I doubt if anyone tells you what to do about anything. Right?"

She answered him with a raised eyebrow and a crooked little smile of her own, but then immediately proceeded to throw him off guard again. "Well, we haven't exactly answered your question, have we?"

"I think I've forgotten the question," he said, his eyes laughing at her.

"You wanted to know when you could see me again," she reminded him.

"Oh—right. Well, I guess I'll just call you over the weekend and we'll work it out, how will that be?"

"Fine. But there's one thing I don't understand," she added, looking at him with a more sober expression.

"What's that?"

"Why do you even want to see me?" Before he could attempt an answer, she continued, her words tumbling out in a rush. "You've made it uncomfortably clear that you don't approve of my job. You don't like the people I work for. You don't trust anyone remotely connected with the Colony. So what am *I*? The object of some kind of investigative experiment or something?"

His eyes met hers, and for just an instant Danni thought he was about to say something very serious. But the amused glint quickly returned. "Could be I'm just cultivating your vote," he said mildly. "On the other hand," he drawled, "I think it might be your nose. Without a doubt, you have the cutest little nose in the county."

And with that, he tapped her lightly on the end of her cute little nose and walked off, leaving Danni, for one of the very few times in her life, absolutely speechless.

7

By ten-thirty that night, Danni was exhausted. But the anniversary edition was off the press and looked good. Everyone on the printing staff was gone, except for her and Add. She gave him a wan smile, turned out the lights and locked the door to her office.

"Your curfew extension is up, Add," she reminded him as they walked outside to the parking lot. "Do you want me to go in with you and explain?"

"Would you mind?" He gave her a grateful look. "If you could just tell my group leader why I'm late—"

"Sure." Danni gave him a warm grin. "That's the least I can do to repay you for sticking with me tonight."

"You work hard, Miss St. John."

"I like what I do," she replied without hesitation. "My dad used to say I have printer's ink in my blood."

The boy nodded as if he understood. "Do your parents live near here?"

Danni was surprised, but pleased. She'd been trying to open the door for more communication with the teenager ever since they'd met, with no success. She was encouraged by his asking her a question not directly related to their work.

"No, they used to live here in Red Oak, but my mother went to live with her sister in Florida after my father died. What about your family, Add?" she asked after a moment.

He shrugged, glancing down at his feet as they continued walking toward the main building. "We don't keep in touch anymore. I haven't been home for a long time."

"Where is home?" Danni asked softly.

"Tuscaloosa."

"Slow down, Add. In case you haven't noticed, my legs didn't grow much!" She pulled at his arm to slow his pace. "What was your name before—you came here, Add? Or would you rather I didn't ask you that?"

"No, that's all right," he replied quietly, immediately pacing his long-legged stride more to Danni's gait. "My life name was Jerry. Jerry Addison."

Danni didn't miss his use of past tense. "Do your folks know you're here?"

He shook his head. "I don't know—probably not. They're divorced. I don't know where my mom is, and my dad wouldn't care where I am even if he knew," he grated bitterly, still not looking at Danni.

"I'm sorry, Add," Danni said sympathetically, hearing the pain he seemed so intent upon hiding.

"It's okay," he muttered defensively, glancing down at her with a flicker of defiance lighting his dark eyes. "I have a *real* family now—right here at the Colony."

"You're happy here, then?"

"Sure I am! It's great!" He looked at her as though he dared her to disagree. "You ought to join us." He waited a moment, then voiced what Danni interpreted as a question. "Everyone wonders why you haven't."

"Well, Add," Danni said, choosing her words very carefully, "I don't think I could do that. This is just a job for me. It really doesn't have anything to do with my relationship with the Lord. I can't change what I believe based on my employment. I've had quite a few jobs, you see, and each of them has been different. But my position with Jesus Christ stays the same—forever."

He gave her a strange look, then glanced around furtively. "They expect you to join the Colony, Miss St. John," he said hurriedly in a hushed tone. "They're going to think it's weird if you don't."

67

"Listen, Add," Danni said firmly as they crossed from the dirt path to a paved sidewalk, "my faith would never allow me to become a member of the Colony. That simply isn't going to happen." She paused a moment, then continued, "Add, what do they teach you here about God?"

The boy darted a surprised, fleeting look in her direction. "Well, they teach us about love . . . and peace . . . and doing good things."

"What about Jesus? Do they teach you about Him, too?"

"What do you mean?"

"Add," Danni framed her words slowly and distinctly, "do you know about the Son of God?"

"What about Him?" he muttered sullenly.

Danni stopped walking and waited for Add to stop as well. When he turned toward her, she said softly, "He loves you. Do they teach you that? Do they teach you that Jesus is God? That He came to live among us so we could see exactly what God is like and how much He cares about us?"

He made a dismissing motion with one hand. "The Christmas story. Yeah, I heard all that when I was little."

"And the Easter story, too. Did you hear about that?"

"What?" His expression took on a glimmer of distrust.

"The story of the cross. Did anyone ever tell you how Jesus allowed Himself to be nailed to a cross? How He suffered the most awful kind of pain hanging there until He died for our sins? For mine—and yours?"

Add swallowed with apparent difficulty but didn't look away from her. "I heard about it. I went to Vacation Bible School a couple of times when I was a kid."

"What did you think of that story, Add?" Danni urged in a soft but intent voice. "Did you believe it?"

"I—I don't remember much about it."

"I see. You . . . don't talk about the cross here at the Colony, then? Not at all?" Danni already knew the answer, but she hoped to plant at least a tiny seed of doubt in his mind.

He looked at her for a long time, and Danni could have wept for the doubt and the confusion and the appeal in his eyes. "Why would anyone do that?"

She didn't understand for a moment. "Why? What do you mean, Add?"

"I mean, *if* He really did it, *why* did He?"

Danni took a deep breath. "Because He loves you. 'For God so loved the world, that He gave his only begotten Son, that whoever believes in Him should not perish, but have eternal life,' " Danni quoted softly.

Add scuffed the toe of his sandal on the concrete and gave a little grunt of scorn. "You talk about Him as though He's real."

"He *is* real, Add!" Danni assured him.

"But He died—"

"Yes," she agreed carefully. "He died. But He didn't stay in the grave, you see. That was just the beginning of things. He rose from the grave. Proved He was master over death. He's alive now. And He always will be alive. Why, He's here with us right now, Add. He goes with me everywhere I go, because I belong to Him. Maybe you can't see Him, but He's here—I can feel His presence. Besides, He promised me He'd be with me forever—that's written in His Word. And He never, ever breaks a promise."

"That doesn't make sense," he mumbled.

"No," Danni agreed thoughtfully. "It doesn't, does it? But let me tell you something, Add, love never does make sense. Don't try to figure it out, because you can't. Love—especially God's kind of perfect love—doesn't have very much to do with common sense or wisdom or understanding. That's why people sometimes find it so hard to accept—because it's so simple they can't comprehend it."

"That may be okay for you, Miss St. John, if you really believe it, but it doesn't have anything to do with me," he said haltingly.

"It has *everything* to do with you, Add," Danni insisted fervently. "You can be His child, too, just as I am. Don't think that because you're here, at the Colony, He isn't aware of you. He knows all about you, and He cares about you, too—a lot more than any family member or friend could ever care."

Encouraged by the glint of interest she thought she saw in his dark, solemn eyes, Danni touched the boy lightly on the arm. "Add, some day you're going to be faced with a choice. The time will come when you'll have to choose between belonging to Jesus, who wants only the best for you, or Satan, who wants to destroy you. That's the most important choice you'll ever make. It's the difference between light and darkness, life and death, heaven and hell. Just . . . think about it, would you?"

Staring at her as though he couldn't understand what she was all about, the boy nodded, then looked away as they entered his dorm foyer. Frustrated by the difficulty in trying to communicate the love of a heavenly Father to a boy who had apparently never known the love of an earthly father, Danni breathed a quick, silent prayer. *Please, Lord, take this special boy to your heart. Somehow show him your wonderful love and goodness. Open his eyes, Lord, to the truth . . . and get him out of here. Please . . . get him out of this place.*

After signing the group leader's information sheet for Add and explaining why he was late, Danni started out the door, longing for home. Her thoughts were on the leftover pizza she'd put in the freezer the night before. Her mouth watered at the prospect of her favorite snack, pizza and freshly squeezed orange juice. In a few moments, she would crash on the couch, eat and read—

"Oh, no!" she moaned, jerking on the strap of her shoulder

bag in irritation when she realized that the file of advertising proposals she wanted to review before morning was still on her desk.

With a tired sigh, she retraced her steps to the *Standard* building. It was almost eleven now, and the grounds of the Colony were in total darkness except for a few security lights scattered across the area. It was so quiet even the cool breeze that came up without warning sounded loud and harsh to her. She glanced up at the starless sky, surprised at how quickly the balmy temperature of the afternoon had turned to a more seasonal chill.

By the time she left her office again with the advertising file tucked securely under her arm, the breeze had become a sharp wind, encouraging her to half-run the distance to her car. She was almost to the long white infirmary building next to the main parking lot when she heard voices coming from the front of the clinic.

Stopping abruptly, she stared for a moment at the men leaving the infirmary. An unidentifiable stab of caution made her duck back against the end of the building to conceal her presence.

Glancing down the straight line of windows, she could see only a dim night light glowing inside. But a security light a few feet away clearly outlined the figures descending the steps. There were four of them, and Danni immediately recognized two as orderlies who worked in the infirmary and the labs. They flanked two other men, both of whom appeared to be quite elderly. The group was apparently on their way to the main building.

Without moving, she peered around the edge of the frame structure, sharply curious about the lifeless, shuffling demeanor of the men being escorted up the walkway. When an unexpected gust of wind came singing through the enormous pines behind the infirmary, causing one of the orderlies to turn and glance in her direction, Danni quickly

71

flattened herself against the building, not daring to breathe, silently praying he wouldn't see her standing there. But he paused only a moment, then turned and continued walking, his white coat flapping in the wind as he mumbled some indistinct comment to the other orderly.

Once they'd entered the building, Danni hurried to her car and practically jumped inside behind the steering wheel. The engine stalled at her first attempt to start it, but finally the car sputtered and groaned to life.

Her mind played with the scene she'd left behind as she drove home. Something about the two elderly men stumbling up the walk hadn't been . . . right. It was nothing she could pinpoint. But something about the episode nagged at her all the way home. After pulling into the driveway, she remained in the car for a moment, gazing at her house. Its yard light glowed cheerfully in front, the night light from within beamed its faint welcome.

Could they have been drunk? she mused. *No, not drunk, just— lifeless. As though they were walking in their sleep.* Somewhere, perhaps from an old and terrible late night television movie, the phrase, "the walking dead," flitted across her consciousness. *Those men had shuffled up that walkway—or been carried up it—as though they were unconscious.* But that was impossible, wasn't it?

8

The house was cold. Danni went straight to the thermostat, grumbling under her breath and wishing she'd left the furnace on when she saw how far the temperature had dropped.

Her hand on the thermostat, she stood still for a moment, instinctively on guard, but not knowing why. There was only silence, except for the loud spluttering and rumbling of the old furnace coming to life. A sudden replay of her first night home, when she'd found the den in such chaos, flashed through her mind.

Everything seemed to be normal. So why did she have this unexpected case of the "creepies"—her mother's word for anxiety attacks? Taking a deep, steadying breath, she began a tour of the house, going from one room to the next, flipping the overhead lights on and off just to reassure herself that all was well. By the time she reached the kitchen, she had found absolutely nothing. She was tempted to stop right there and ease the hunger gnawing so persistently at her stomach. But she felt grimy and tired and wanted a shower before anything else.

Leaving the kitchen, she returned to the hall and flipped on the upstairs light. Taking the steps two at a time, she shook her head at her own foolishness, dismissing her earlier jitters.

After a hurried shower, she slipped into the creamy peach velour robe her mother had sent her for her last birthday, then walked over to her dressing table. She dropped to her knees, but as usual, the hateful bottom drawer refused to open until she grasped firmly on both handles and tugged back, full-force, almost tipping over in the effort. She retrieved a small cassette recorder hidden beneath a pile of seldom-worn nightgowns, pushed a top button for a quick battery check, and started to force the cantankerous drawer shut.

A small piece of silver metal caught her eye. She rolled it between two fingers as she puzzled over what it might be and how it could have gotten into the drawer. She glanced from the piece of metal to the recorder, but nothing appeared broken or missing. Getting to her feet, she held the metal up to the light for a better look, rubbing it between her thumb and index finger several times. Whatever it was, it didn't belong to her. Finally giving up on identifying it, she dropped it into one pocket of her robe and gave the drawer a final, exasperated shove with her foot. Much to her surprise, it closed with a resounding bang.

Feeling her earlier tension drape itself across her shoulders, she pushed the record switch and began to walk across the bedroom, speaking into the recorder as she walked. Her words were somewhat rushed as she detailed the events of the day, concentrating on the strange scenario she'd observed at the Colony earlier that evening. Going to stand by the window, she glanced down idly at the stately Georgian dollhouse which stood on a walnut stand that had been custom built for it.

Pushing the pause button on the recorder, she nudged an edge of floral drapery away from the window to look out, surprised to see the taillights of a car that appeared to be pulling away from the curb in front of her house. She moved quickly to the center of the window, trying to get a better look at the vehicle, but it was already out of her view.

Danni dropped the small recorder into the pocket of her robe and stood staring out the window for a moment. Where had the car come from? It hadn't been there when she pulled into the driveway, she was positive.

Shaken, she moved away from the window. Walking around to the back of the dollhouse, she picked up a porcelain doll in a frivolous lace ballgown from where it had toppled over onto the living room floor of the house.

"Sorry, Cassandra, dear—you seem to have bumped your head," Danni said distractedly. She carefully returned the doll to its former position on the piano bench. Just that morning, in the throes of a playful mood, she'd placed her there before going downstairs for breakfast.

She turned to leave the room, still thinking about the car she'd seen, when she stopped, lifted her chin, and waited. Thinking. Thinking about the dollhouse. Something else had been out of place . . . .

Danni whirled around and walked back to the dollhouse, leaning over enough to allow herself a good view of the inside. It took her a moment, but she found what she was looking for. Not only had the doll fallen over, but in the bedroom directly overhead, a lamp from the miniature night table was on the floor and a tiny platform rocker was lying on its side.

Logan hadn't been far from the truth when he'd accused Danni of being a "little girl at heart" the evening he'd been there for dinner. Indeed, at twenty-seven, Danni had a great deal of little girl fantasy within her. But it was a personality trait that had never much bothered her. She enjoyed her dollhouses and often moved her "people" and their furniture around to suit her mood.

But coupled with her childish sense of wonder was a meticulous attention to these miniature homes. Had anyone asked, she could have run down a detailed list of room settings and people placement for any given dollhouse in her collection at any time. She might not remember where she'd put the tennis shoes she'd been wearing the day before—but she knew precisely what was what and who was where among her miniature families.

And that was exactly what was bothering her now. In addition to the car she'd just seen and the piece of metal in her drawer, she added the toppled doll, the fallen lamp, and the tumbled rocker. They hadn't been that way earlier.

The leftover pizza was put on hold. The fresh orange juice was temporarily forgotten. She wandered about the bedroom, her mind moving swiftly from one possibility to another, then discarding all of them. She retrieved the recorder from her pocket. Pulling out the small piece of silver metal along with it, she glanced from it to the dollhouse, then again to the palm of her hand. Flipping on the record switch, she made a quick note to the recorder that she believed someone had been in the house during her absence. That completed, she returned the recorder to its place beneath the mound of expensive lingerie her Aunt Kathryn insisted upon sending her for her hope chest.

Standing, she turned to stare with dread at the open bedroom door. If she didn't inspect the other three bedrooms off the long, narrow hallway, she wouldn't close her eyes tonight. But the thought of facing the cold, waiting darkness of the unused rooms intimidated her more than she cared to admit. *Oh, for goodness sake, St. John, get a grip on yourself! If anyone was still in the house, he'd have made himself known before now!*

Finally, she willed herself to leave the room and creep cautiously down the hall. When she reached the first bedroom, she gently nudged the door open and with trembling fingers flipped the wall switch, bathing the room with light. Stepping just inside, she peered around the large room, sighing with relief when she saw its massive, late-Victorian furniture undisturbed.

She turned off the light and quietly closed the door, glancing directly across the hall to what had been her parents' bedroom. Hesitating only an instant, she crossed to open the door and fumbled for the light switch, only to remember that this room had no overhead lighting. Her jaw clamped tight with tension, she walked resolutely into the dark room. Slowly she felt her way around the enormous Renaissance bed in search of the washstand which held a glass-globed lamp. Turning the key-shaped switch, she let her gaze travel about the dimly lighted room.

At once she sensed something wrong. Danni felt her skin tingle and her heart thud as she walked to the end of the bed where she discovered corners of fabric hanging from the closed lid of a blanket chest.

She wiped her damp palms down the sides of her robe a few times before raising the hinged top of the chest to stare down into what she was sure had once been neat stacks of linens and bedding. The contents had been riffled and strewn.

She lowered the lid slowly and stood rigidly still. Unwillingly she scanned the rest of the room, her eyes now accustomed to the dim lighting. Heaps of clothing had been randomly tossed to the floor from the open drawers of a tall bureau; papers were scattered about on the floor beside a sloping-front desk; and the doors of a double wardrobe stood open, revealing piles of clothing stripped thoughtlessly from their hangers.

Danni felt her heart skip a beat, then pump erratically, as a soft moan escaped her lips. Unable to move, she stared with sick fixation at the disheveled room around her, feeling herself once more to be the victim of some nameless, faceless intruder. Pressing the back of her hand against her mouth to choke off the cry that threatened to explode, she took one last horrified look around the room before realizing she might not be alone.

With movements as stiff and uncoordinated as a marionette, she ran from the room, frantically seeking the haven of her bedroom. Wheezing, with the familiar cold perspiration dotting her forehead, she slammed the door shut behind her. She stared for a long moment at the old fashioned keyhole lock below the porcelain doorknob before making the swift decision to turn the key.

She moved hesitantly toward the marble top stand beside her bed, staring at the telephone. Every instinct wanted to call Logan, but a mixture of pride and indecision made her hesitate. When it shrilled while she was still trying to make a decision, she nearly screamed, grabbing it so quickly she almost knocked it off the stand.

"Danni?" She could have gone to her knees with relief. It was Logan. *Thank You, Lord!* "Danni—are you okay?"

How, she wondered irrationally, could such a big man, a man who seemed to spend a great deal of time looking mean or at the least woefully disgusted, and who appeared to be set on making a part-time career of knocking the wind out of her sails—how could that same man possibly have such a wonderfully endearing and so very welcome voice?

"I—Logan? Hello?"

"I was getting a little worried. I called several times and didn't get any answer."

She wondered if he could hear the trembling in her voice. "Oh . . . yes. Well, I haven't been home very long. I had to work even later than I'd expected."

There was a moment of silence before he answered. "Just wanted to be sure," he said softly. "I was worried about you being out there so late."

"Oh . . ." she replied lamely. "Well—it's nice of you to be—concerned about that." She raised her eyes upward with a silent groan. *How did you ever make it as a writer, ninny? This conversation is not exactly award material.*

"Ah . . . Logan? You weren't here—earlier—were you?"

"At your house? No. When?"

"Oh—well, a car pulled away from the curb a few minutes ago, and I couldn't see who it was. Not that there was any reason for me to think it was you," she added hastily. "I just thought—"

"You didn't see who was driving?" he interrupted.

"No, I couldn't even be sure where it came from. But it looked as though it had been parked in front of the house and after—"

"After what?"

Danni fumbled for her glasses, but when she didn't find them on top of her head, she stopped looking. "Nothing."

"Something's wrong. What?" His voice had taken on its familiar note of irritated urgency now.

"Well . . . someone's been in the house."

"How do you know?" he snapped.

"I wasn't sure at first. A couple of things weren't the way I thought I'd left them this morning—in my bedroom. So I decided I'd better check the rest of the upstairs. My parents' bedroom—well, everything in it is a mess. Someone—"

He broke into her faltering sentence, announcing curtly, "I'm coming in."

"No, Logan! I didn't mean that you should—"

"Where are you?" he questioned shortly, ignoring her weak protest.

"What do you mean? I'm at home, of course, where do you think—"

He sighed, a sound of exaggerated patience. "Where in the *house* are you?"

"Oh. I'm upstairs. In my room. Why?"

"Does the door have a lock?"

"Does it have—yes. I've locked it already."

"Good. You stay right where you are until I get there. I'm at home. It'll take me about fifteen minutes."

"Logan, I've been through almost the entire house, and there is no one—" She swallowed hard, letting her words fall away, feeling a subtle chill snake its way down her spine.

"Probably not. But humor me. Don't leave your bedroom

until I get there." He hung up without saying good-bye, leaving Danni to stare wordlessly at the receiver in her hand. After replacing it with a loud thump, she glanced over at the door, unable to keep herself from wondering if she *was* alone in the house.

At last she made herself move, trading her robe for a worn pair of jeans and a rumpled big shirt. A glance in the mirror told her her hair needed combed—and she wished she hadn't washed off the little makeup she'd been wearing—but what difference did it make? The man was too busy playing cops and robbers to pay any attention to her appearance anyway. Not that she cared.

She wished he'd hurry. Remembering the car she'd seen pulling away, she was sure there was no one in the house, but still . . . she hadn't checked the other bedroom at the end of the hall. But certainly with all the noise she'd made during the last half hour, if anyone was waiting—

Danni swallowed hard, choking on what felt like a huge knot in her throat. Crossing her arms over her chest and rubbing her shoulders distractedly, she paced back and forth, alert to every tiny creak or shudder around her.

When she finally heard Logan's heavy pounding downstairs, she practically tore the bedroom door off the frame getting it unlocked. She charged down the stairs and yanked the heavy front door open, as Logan yelled her name for the third time. Pulling herself up to as much height as she could muster, Danni began to protest. "Will you stop *screaming* at me, for goodness sake—"

9

He ignored her outburst and gently pushed her back as he walked inside. "Have you checked every room?" He asked tersely, moving toward the living room, flipping light switches as he went.

"Please, do come in, Logan," Danni said dryly.

Infuriatingly indifferent to her, he tossed his leather jacket over a chair and kept right on walking, leaving Danni to scurry along behind him toward the kitchen. "How long have you been home?"

"About half an hour, but—"

He turned to face her and it occurred to Danni that he didn't look quite so big and nasty in jeans and a sweatshirt as he did in uniform, especially with his hair windblown. Unconsciously, she raised a hand to her own tousled hair.

His eyes followed her movement. "Besides the mess in your parents' room, what else is out of place?"

Danni drew in a deep breath. She'd expected him to ask that, yet wished he hadn't. "Some pieces in my dollhouse— the one in my bedroom." She stopped, embarrassed, anticipating his derision.

But he simply waited, his dark gaze moving over her face, revealing no hint of laughter.

Surprised as well as relieved, Danni continued. "You see, I remembered where Cassandra—that's the mother of the dollhouse family—was this morning. She was playing the piano. But tonight she was lying on the floor. And the rocking chair and a lamp in the bedroom had fallen over, too."

"In the dollhouse," he repeated tonelessly.

"Yes. I know you probably don't understand this, but I always know exactly where things are. In the dollhouses, that is. I never know where *anything* else is. Anyway, things were *not* the way I left them this morning." She came up for air, then added, "And then I saw the car—"

He nodded, and Danni was encouraged to see that he was apparently taking her seriously. "I could really use a cup of coffee," he said. "Would you want to make some while I check the rooms upstairs?"

She could hear him walking around above her, thumping things and banging doors, and she found the sounds strangely reassuring. By the time he returned to the kitchen, the coffee was done, and Danni had scooped some peanut butter cookies out of the Victorian Lady cookie jar on the counter and arranged them on a tray.

"Other than the mess they made, I didn't find a thing," he told her, eyeing with interest the cookies she'd set out. "Mmm."

"My way of thanking you for coming to my rescue," Danni said. "And apologizing—for being such a grouch," she explained when he lifted a questioning brow.

Straddling a chair, he consumed half a cookie in one bite, glancing at the other half in his hand. "Impressive." Then he smiled. "I was ready for your grouch routine. It's after eleven."

"What?" She stared at him dumbly.

"You're a night grouch. You were really bad your first night back in town," he explained in response to her puzzled look. "I figure it's got something to do with your bio-rhythms."

"If it does," she said sweetly, "yours must have bounced right off the scale that night." As she went back to the counter for cream and sugar, she added, "Anyway, I'm sorry you drove all the way over here for nothing."

He shook his head. "I didn't. Look what I got for my trouble," he said, taking another cookie.

"I do appreciate your coming, Logan, even if it wasn't necessary." She sat down in the chair opposite him.

"Well," he replied, a faint twinkle dancing in his eyes, "If I want to see you, I have to take advantage of the situations as they come, I s'pose."

Unsettled by the measuring look that punctuated his words, Danni awkwardly returned his smile and reached for a cookie. They traded small talk for a few moments before Logan's mood abruptly darkened.

"Danni, is there any particular reason why someone would ransack your house?" He watched her carefully.

"No. I can't think of a—" Suddenly another thought occurred to her, and with it came a distinct feeling of apprehension.

"Logan—how do you suppose they got in?"

"Easy," he replied. "Your bedroom window was unlocked."

Her eyes widened. "But that's two stories up—"

"With a monster of a tree leanin' right up against it," he finished for her.

Dismayed, she stared back at him. "But it wasn't my room they tore apart—"

"I know," he said thoughtfully, "but someone was in it, that's for sure. Maybe they got nervous and took off before they were done. I had that phone ringin' off the hook for quite awhile. Maybe they were afraid someone would show up to see about you. But I wonder why they trashed your parents' bedroom?"

She shook her head, honestly bewildered. "I have no idea. There's nothing in that room except some old clothes my mother didn't want—her own, my dad's—even some of my things."

"Well, someone might be trying to scare you, but I don't really think that's what this is all about."

"What *do* you think?" she asked, trying to subdue the disturbing little shivers of fear darting along her spine.

"I get the feeling," he said slowly, "that someone thinks you have something they want. Or," he mused thoughtfully, not looking at her, "maybe they're just trying to find out something about you." When he lifted his eyes to meet hers, Danni was sure she could see the questions playing at his mind. "Are you certain there was nothing else out of place—or missing?"

"No, noth—oh! Wait a minute," Danni said slowly, remembering the small piece of metal she'd found in the bottom dresser drawer. "I *did* find something, but I don't think it has anything to do with—"

"What was it?" he interrupted.

When she told him, he sent her upstairs to get it. She returned quickly, handing it to him. "Can you tell what it is?"

He examined it closely, rolling it around the palm of his hand a few times. "Why do I think it's something familiar?" he murmured, holding it up to the light. "Let me keep it, okay? Maybe it'll come to me." He stuck it down in the pocket of his jeans. "Where did you say you found it?"

"In my bottom dresser drawer."

"What else do you keep in there?"

Danni colored slightly and stiffened, not wanting to tell him about the recorder—or the lingerie. "Ah . . . nothing special."

He gave her a peculiar look, then grinned as though something had just dawned on him. But he asked simply, "Nothing else?"

The flush creeping up her face deepened. "No . . . nothing important."

"Well, I think you need to be careful," he said firmly, his expression sobering as he leaned back and folded his arms over his chest. "And," he added sternly, "I want you to promise you'll call me if you even think you've got trouble. If I'm not in town, I'm out at the farm." He ignored her attempted protest. "And if for some reason you can't find me, get in touch with Phil Rider. He'll help you out."

Danni was surprised that the thought of asking Logan's cousin for help made her feel oddly uncomfortable. "Logan—" She was hesitant about mentioning the idea that had been growing in the back of her mind for days now, but decided since he'd given her such an excellent opportunity, she might just as well pursue it. "About being careful—didn't you tell me you teach karate at the high school?" She reached for his cup and got up to refill it.

He nodded, his forehead creasing to a small frown of puzzlement.

"Well, I've been thinking . . . I'd like to learn how to defend myself," she told him, returning with his coffee and sitting down across from him again. "Will you teach me?"

For one long moment, Danni thought he was going to laugh at her, but he must have thought better of it. However, his mumbled, "no way," was flat and definite.

"What do you mean, *no way*?" she countered indignantly. "I'll come to class just like anyone else. I'll pay you, I don't expect any free favors."

"*If* I were willing to take you on as a student," he interrupted, "you *would* pay. But the answer is no." He rose from the chair and went to stand at the counter, leaning casually against it as he faced her.

"Would you mind telling me why? I could learn just as quickly as anyone else and you know it!"

His easy smile infuriated her. "Oh, I don't doubt that for a minute. That's not the problem."

When he showed no sign of explaining, Danni glared up at him, her eyes burning with challenge. "Then what *is* the problem?"

He took a long, leisurely sip of coffee before he answered.

"I think," he drawled, "that with your particular combination of stubbornness and tunnel vision—not to mention your temper—a few lessons in karate might turn you into a lethal weapon." Looking her squarely in the eye, he grinned as though he were enjoying himself immensely. "See, what I'm afraid of is that I'd be creating a monster that might get out of control."

Danni growled under her breath, sputtered, and hurled a look at him that would have flattened a weaker man. But her tight, furious mask gradually dropped away as she watched his smug expression turn to laughter. "You're not serious," she said slowly, awareness dawning on her.

"I wasn't," he admitted. "But now I am," he added quickly with a glint of warning in his eyes. "You tell me why you think you might need to defend yourself and we'll talk about some lessons."

"I should think," Danni said stiffly, "that no law enforcement officer would need to ask that question of anyone in today's world."

"Spare me the decent-law-abiding-citizen's lecture," he returned lightly. "You haven't answered my question."

"I just want to learn, that's all!" she insisted sharply. "*You're* the one who's scaring me half to death with your warnings about being careful and—"

"You could always get a dog," he commented blandly, ignoring her scowl. "Besides, aren't you afraid of compromising your faith?"

Danni's head reeled at the quick change of subject. "What are you talking about?"

He shrugged. "Some people don't believe in martial arts."

"Why? It's just a method of self-defense."

"It is. But it can still come down to a form of combat, given a threatening situation."

She thought about this for a moment. "I don't think it's

86

wrong to know how to defend yourself. Or help someone else who's in trouble."

His expression hardened. "Not everyone is comfortable with that perspective. It's a lot easier to plead ignorance—do nothing."

Danni saw resentment flicker in his eyes and heard the edge of cynicism in his voice. "Why do I get the feeling you're talking about more than karate?" she asked softly.

Logan looked at her thoughtfully. "I probably am," he admitted.

"Tell me," she prompted.

He shook his head. "I don't think so. You probably wouldn't agree with me anyway."

"Sometimes . . . I think you're awfully hard on people, Logan," she said slowly. "You seem to expect a lot—maybe more than they're capable of giving. Does that have anything to do with being a sheriff?"

"No," he tossed back in an unexpectedly harsh tone. "It has more to do with the fact that I see too many people hiding in their own foggy little apathetic corners until something threatens their neat and tidy existence. By the time they start yelling for action, the battle's usually over."

Stunned by the unexpected force of his retort, Danni could do nothing but stare at him.

"I'm sorry," he muttered, not looking at her. "We should have left it alone."

"Am I included in that generalization you just made?"

He hesitated only a moment. "Let's clear the air between us, Danni. I don't like the people you work for—any of them. And I don't pretend to understand why you got yourself mixed up with that outfit—"

He raised a hand and shook his head to stop her attempted protest. "I don't *have* to understand, I s'pose. Who you work for is your business. But I *do* want you to know where I'm coming from on this. The Colony of the Lotus"—his tone sounded deliberately nasty—"has changed this whole town, and a good many lives." He took a deep sip of coffee and stared down at the floor for a moment.

When he continued, his voice was somewhat softer but still firm with conviction. "They're up to some weird stuff out there. I can't prove it yet—but I know it, just the same. And for the last two years, they've been moving into areas very few people know anything about. They're making subtle little inroads into some very important places. Frankly, they scare me to death. That's right," he affirmed quickly when he saw her surprised expression. "They scare me. They have, right from the beginning."

His eyes narrowed, and Danni could actually feel the anger rising in him. "But let me tell you what bothers me a lot more than Reverend Ra and his little robots. This town is full of good people—many of them Christians—who sat back on their indifference and threw the city gate wide open for that corrupt little kingdom out there. A couple of other people—who are no longer residents, by the way, since their homes got burned down—went with me to the city council to try to stop the initial group who came in here and bought the Gunderson land." He rubbed a hand down one side of his beard irritably, as though the memory still grated on him.

Leaning wearily against the counter again, he continued. "Rumor says the Gundersons were paid three times what that property was worth. Anyway—it was a private sale and council wouldn't even discuss the change they made in the zoning restrictions to accommodate the new owners. I s'pose the prospect of all that increased revenue for the town coffers—which has never materialized, incidentally—was just too appealing."

"When we gave up on the council," he said, his tone still thick with resentment, "we went to the churches. All of them. Tried to convince them of what these people were, what could happen if they weren't stopped. I did my homework, Danni," he assured her quietly. "Before I ever talked with the first person, I made it my business to know what I was talking *about*." He shook his head, and Danni thought she could see a trace of the disillusionment that he must have experienced during that time.

"You know what we heard from the churches? From most of them, anyway? They said they couldn't get involved. That it really wasn't any of their business—it was for the city council to handle. A couple of the ministers who wanted to keep them out made a stand. But it wasn't enough." He walked away from the counter to look out the glass pane of the back door. "It's true, you know, that old saying, 'The only thing necessary for the triumph of evil is for good men to do nothing'."

He turned back to her. "That's exactly what happened in Red Oak. Everybody was so busy watching their television shows and going to Bible studies and fellowship dinners and committee meetings, they couldn't be bothered to take on the devil. So he just moved right on in and took up permanent residence. The Colony got their land. Then they built their buildings and brought in their 'converts,' and their 'teachers,' and now they're bringing in their elderly 'guests.' It would seem," he said softly, "that there's just no stopping them."

And then he looked at her again, and something inside of him seemed to stop. He drew in a deep breath.

"We could have kept it from happening. Just a little support from the town leaders would have done it. Now . . . it's probably too late. And I hate that. Because they just keep bringing in their evil—more and more of it. They're eventually going to own this town—and the county, most likely. They'll destroy whatever is good about it and replace it with their own kind of garbage. And there doesn't seem to be one thing I can do about it."

He shoved his hands deep into his pockets and glanced around the kitchen. "You know, I love this town. And in my own way, I s'pose I love the people. But I don't understand them," he said, shaking his head. "I simply do not understand why they let it happen."

A small, uneasy twitch jumped at the corner of Danni's left eye as she studied his face. "I suppose," she said in a small voice, "you think I'm terrible. For working there."

He stood very still, looking down at the floor for a long time. When he lifted his gaze to hers again, Danni was surprised to see that all the anger and every trace of resentment was gone from his features. He wore only an odd little smile and a look she hadn't seen before in his eyes, a look that might have bordered on tenderness. "I'm afraid I would have a whole lot of trouble," he said softly, "convincing myself that you're a terrible person."

Their gazes locked and held, a feeling passing between them that seemed to unsettle one as much as the other. Danni fumbled for words. "That's—why you don't go to church anymore, isn't it?" Her voice was low and uncertain.

For a moment she thought he wasn't going to answer. But he did, and she saw confusion in his eyes. "I s'pose it is, yes." Something dim and shaded darkened his gaze. "I can't seem to handle it, at least not right now. I tried . . . for awhile. I went and I listened and I watched everyone, but then I'd think about the way they turned their backs on something so obviously evil—" His words drifted off, and he lifted his shoulders in a small, questioning shrug.

"Logan . . . I think I understand what you're saying . . . and why you feel the way you do. But don't you think you need to find just a little tolerance, maybe even some forgiveness, for these people?"

His hard, closed look very nearly silenced her. It was only the pain she had sensed in him, the festering, gnawing pain that was so often the unexpected problem child of bitterness that made her press. "It sounds trite . . . but they're only human. They didn't realize what their indifference would lead to."

"And most of them still don't," he grated harshly. "They're as blind as they were then, and they're not going to wake up until it's too late. Until some of their own kids have been destroyed by that—" He stopped abruptly. "I'm sorry. I didn't mean to get into this. Let's drop it."

"Logan, it's all right. I understand." Danni cleared her throat and purposely attempted to change the tone of their conversation. "About the karate lessons—"

He stared at her in disbelief, then chuckled, raising his arms in a gesture of defeat. "Okay, I give. Be there at four next Tuesday. On Thursdays the sessions are for high school students only. But Tuesday I'm starting a new series for the public. It's open to anyone who registers that day." He grinned wickedly. "And don't forget your deposit—twenty-five dollars."

She lifted a skeptical eyebrow and asked dryly, "How much for the entire session?"

He seemed to consider her question carefully for a moment. "Well, now, let's see. Maybe we can make a trade."

"Like what?" She was suspicious of any favors he might be offering.

He grinned as though he knew she was expecting the worst. "I'll take ten percent off the total if you'll write me a good campaign speech. Twenty percent off if you'll have dinner with me tomorrow night."

Danni's mouth dropped open, but she recovered quickly. "The speech might be a possibility. But you said you have to work tomorrow night."

"I'm off at eight."

"All the restaurants in Red Oak are probably closed by nine."

"We'll eat fast," he insisted.

She might as well agree. The truth of the matter was she wanted to be with him. The question was *why.*

"All right. Now, I want to be sure I understand you correctly. If I go out with you tomorrow night *and* write a speech for you, I'll get thirty percent off the total cost of the lessons."

"I didn't say that—"

"Oh, but you did, *Sheriff.* Ten for the speech, twenty for dinner. That makes thirty. Do we have a deal or not?"

He laced the fingers of both hands together in front of him. "I don't suppose you'd want to try for fifty percent?"

Her withering glare was all the reply he needed. "Right. We stop with thirty. I'll pick you up a little after eight—okay?"

Just before he went out the front door, he turned back to her, studying her face with an expression Danni hadn't seen before. He laid one large hand lightly upon her narrow shoulder, his eyes searching hers. "Don't take any dumb chances, Half-pint," he commanded. "Something about this thing with your house bothers me. A lot. Give me a chance to put it together, okay? In the meantime, be careful."

She had lost her fight, and along with it any desire to toss out a flippant remark. "I'll be fine, Logan."

He gave her shoulder one final squeeze. "I intend to make sure of that," he said softly. "Good night, now."

10

A strong rush of nostalgia assailed Danni as she walked down the hushed, tiled hallway she had known during her high school years. It was quiet now, but she could almost hear the clamor of loud, excited voices from years before as she remembered jostling around the lockers with her friends, hurrying between bells to catch the latest gossip or dump some books before picking up more.

After changing into the brand new white *gi* she'd bought for her first class, she entered the gymnasium, her mood lifting somewhat. Even though she felt a little foolish, appearing in front of strangers barefoot in the loose-fitting, drawstring pants and long-sleeved top that reminded her of pajamas, she sailed through the double doors with confidence, prepared to toss a dazzling smile at the instructor—who was nowhere in sight.

Disappointed, she stood close to the gym wall, studying the other students in the room while she waited. There were about a dozen, both men and women. Some stood around in small groups chatting, a few others were doing what appeared to be warm-up exercises.

A slender blond man who looked to be in his late twenties walked up to her with a welcoming smile. He introduced himself as Logan's assistant and a science teacher at the high school.

Danni wished Logan would hurry. Not only was she anxious to show him that she meant business by showing up early for this first class, but she hadn't seen him since they'd gone out to dinner on Saturday night.

It hadn't been much of a date, she thought with a grim

smile. Logan hadn't been able to get free until after nine o'clock, so they'd settled for pizza at Miller's, where they'd spent most of an hour and a half preparing an outline for a campaign speech. He was not an easy man to draw information from. He seemed to think things like speeches and slogans were only for Washington, and his idea of a platform was a square piece of wood.

"Well, what are you *running* on?" Danni had finally demanded in desperation, wondering how any man who appeared so shrewd could possibly be so dense.

"A very low budget," he'd replied soberly, glancing up from his Personal Deep-Dish Supreme Pizza Delight when she growled and threatened to make him wear his dinner. She had finally given up after asking who would be the victims of this speech, only to learn that there was no intended audience. He simply wanted something to keep on file for possible use later on in the campaign.

"Hah! This, Logan McGarey, is not a campaign you're running," she declared spitefully. "You're erecting your own deadfall!"

He grinned while she fumed, and then he reached across the table with his enormous red and white napkin to wipe away a string of mozzarella from her chin, making it very difficult for Danni to continue haranguing him.

Still, she'd been able to come up with enough information to construct a rough draft. She'd brought it with her tonight, hoping he'd have time to go over it before she went to work on a final copy.

When one of the gym doors banged shut, Danni whirled around. Her eyes widened when she saw Logan enter, attired in the uniform white *gi*, a black belt draped casually at his waist. Even though she felt conspicuously absurd in her own outfit, she had to give the man his due. Barefoot and all, he was a dark, dazzling contrast to his white apparel.

She stared at him with guarded appreciation, grinning as

she waited for him to notice her. She was certain he did—he looked directly at her. But when he didn't so much as allow a flicker of recognition to pass between them, Danni began a slow simmer of annoyance and disappointment.

Only once did she catch a glimpse of what might have been a smile in his eyes, shortly after he'd started them on their warm-ups to "loosen their joints" and "stretch those seldom-used muscles." By then Danni had woefully decided that her joints were permanently cemented and a number of her muscles had apparently never been used. *So go ahead and ignore me, Brave Eagle—and write your own campaign speeches while you're at it!*

Danni prided herself on being in reasonably good shape. She wasn't a runner, and she wasn't big on any particular physical fitness routine, but she did walk often, occasionally went to the Y to swim, and kept her weight within two or three pounds of what it was supposed to be. At the moment, however, she felt more like a glob of Super Glue. Her only consolation was that very few of the others in the class appeared to be faring any better.

Only their tall, dark *sensei*—she'd learned that Logan was referred to by the Japanese title for teacher—was at ease and obviously enjoying himself as he watched this brutal misuse of all the human body was ever intended for. He and his assistant, Mark Clifford, weren't even breathing hard as they participated in the warm-ups.

Danni spitefully decided to ask Logan later on how a man *his age* endured this kind of punishment. However, when she grudgingly reminded herself that this was, after all, her own idea, and that Logan was only doing what he was paid to do—and doing it very well—she gave herself a mental slap on the hands and set about getting her money's worth. But she shuddered involuntarily when she realized that she hadn't even made it past the preliminary stuff yet.

When they finally reached the end of the leg stretches

and sit-ups, Danni was convinced that none of this was for her. She had come with the intention of learning to defend herself, and instead she was killing herself. The only thing that kept her from walking—no, running—out of the gym was the knowledge that she'd have to face Logan again eventually. So she stayed.

She stayed and was initiated into the techniques of the attention stance and the horseback stance and the cat stance. She learned about high blocks and low blocks and middle blocks. She practiced the karate shout, deciding it was easily the most manageable technique among all this craziness, and it gave her a nasty little sense of satisfaction to use it every time Logan came close to her. She was also given a first-hand demonstration of punches and strikes, front kicks and side kicks, high kicks and round kicks and elbow attacks. Above all she began to understand pain—real physical pain, galvanizing, agonizing neck pain and back pain and leg pain.

She refused to acknowledge to herself that the sudden acceleration of her heartbeat when Logan circled her waist gently with his large hands to show her how to bend and block had anything to do with his nearness or his touch. After all, she was exhausted, wasn't she? The thundering pulse she seemed to have developed was most likely the result of extreme fatigue and utter frustration.

Just before the class was due to end, Logan brought everything to a halt and spent a few minutes t lking with them. Danni was struck, not for the first time, by the inescapable magnetism of the man. He seemed to charge the very air around them with a sharp current of energy, even though his manner was usually very laid-back and casual. As she had in the past, she wondered about this enigma of a man who could, she suspected, cower the hardest of criminals, and yet turn unexpectedly gentle at the least likely moment.

And her own reaction to him puzzled her every bit as much as his attitude toward her. She spent most of her time in his presence wanting to give in to the temptation to thump him on the head. But there were those few unsettling moments when she warmed to the smile in his eyes and delighted in his soft, deep-pitched laugh or his light, fleeting touch on her shoulder. And Danni wasn't so sure that the perplexing sheriff didn't have his own share of conflicting emotions where she was concerned. She'd caught him staring at her more than once with an expression that hinted of some unfamiliar depth of feeling, although most often his look was one of indulgent amusement. It should worry her, she supposed, that lately she'd even found herself reading a touch of tenderness into his patronizing sneer.

She forced herself back to her surroundings, turning her attention to Logan's words. "I've already told you that *karate* means 'open hand.' You become your own defensive weapon. This class is going to stress defense only. My reason for working with you is not so that you can hurt someone. It's simply so you can keep yourself from becoming a victim."

His eyes narrowed slightly as he went on. "But you have to remember one thing. Reaction is all-important with karate— just as it is with a lot of other things in life. You wait too long, and you lose the moment. It won't work for you. There's a point in time when you have the advantage, when you have the opportunity to overcome." His stare was hard and commanding as he made deliberate eye contact, one by one, with each person in the room. "If you don't react when you should, if you wait too long, then you invite defeat.

"Sometimes," he added after a noticeable pause, "you can't avoid confrontation. That's when it's essential that you make the right choices, at exactly the right time. Hopefully, this class will help you learn how to do that."

His tone lightened abruptly. "Earlier this evening, some of

you requested a demonstration. If you like, Mark and I will run through a few brief techniques before you leave."

It occurred to Danni, as she watched the two men bow to each other and begin their exhibition, that Logan, with all his rhythmic grace and fluid movement, could undeniably become a lethal weapon once unleashed.

She stood unmoving, her mouth slightly agape, as the men threw lightning quick punches and blocked expertly with perfect balance. The dull "thwack" of their blows echoed through the gym. The ends of Logan's black belt swirled loosely about his slim waist as his movements grew faster, his hands slicing the air with almost invisible strikes, his powerful shoulders tightening and easing beneath the white material, his long legs dancing in a flowing but unpredictable pattern of finesse.

Her irritation with him disappeared. It faded into admiration and still another unfamiliar emotion which threatened to make her lose her composure when, the demonstration ended and the class dismissed, he approached her.

"Cute," he said dryly, his eyes twinkling as he assessed Danni from head to toe. "You look about fourteen in that *gi*, Half-pint."

"Believe me, *sensei*," she grated nastily, "I feel a lot more than fourteen right now! More like a hundred."

"Ah," he drawled with patently fake concern, "suffering, are you?"

"Would you really like to know how I feel, Logan?"

He laughed. "I think I'm familiar with most of the standard complaints. Just wait till tomorrow morning—it gets worse."

She groaned. "Maybe I should just buy a dog, like you suggested."

"You're not going to give up that easily?" he countered.

"I'll let you know tomorrow."

He touched her shoulder lightly. "I've been meaning to

ask you . . . do you have plans for Thanksgiving Day?"

"Thanksgiving Day?" Danni repeated, frowning slightly.

"It's day after tomorrow, remember?" he said, smiling at her obvious lapse of memory.

She lightly smacked the side of her head with the open palm of one hand. "I can't *believe* that! I'd forgotten all about it!"

"Good, then you're free. I thought maybe you could come out to the farm and have dinner with Tucker and me."

"Tucker?"

"Oh, that's right—you haven't met Tucker yet, have you? Tucker Wells. He's what the old plantation owners would have called an overseer, I s'pose. 'Course, I don't have a plantation—just a little farm—so I'm not sure what his title is. But he takes care of the place for me. Does a little of everything, including the cooking. Otherwise I'd probably starve." Another thought seemed to strike him, and his smile widened. "Listen—would you really like to have a dog?"

She stared at him for a moment. "A dog—well, sure, I guess. Could I forget the karate lessons if I did, do you think?"

He shook his head in mock disillusionment. "I'm surprised at you. Do you know," he said, a glimmer of mischief lighting his eyes, "that there's a ninety-year old lady in the midwest who just earned her black belt?"

Danni hesitated only a moment, then fanned her eyelashes ingenuously. "That's a great idea, *sensei*," she cooed. "I'll see you in about sixty-three years, okay?"

He laughed delightedly at her. "About the dog. Sassy—she's my Irish setter—had eight puppies a couple of weeks ago. If you'd really like to have a dog, you can pick out the one you want Thursday, and when it's weaned, it's all yours." He grinned. "They're good Irish stock, I guarantee it."

"Mm. Like you, I suppose."

His smile weakened unexpectedly and he glanced away

from her. "If you want to take advantage of the showers, they're in there," he said flatly, pointing to a door behind Danni.

Surprised by his quick change of subject, she nodded. "I know. I went to school here. About Thanksgiving—I'd love to come, if you really want me to. What can I bring?"

"Absolutely nothing but yourself," he said firmly, his smile returning. "But I'll come and get you, so you don't have to drive back alone that night. We probably won't eat until after six."

"Oh, you don't have to do that. I'm used to driving in alone from the Colony—"

"I'll pick you up about five," he said in a tone that finalized the conversation.

"Well, all right. Oh—I have a draft of your speech with me, by the way. Why don't we just wait until Thursday evening and go over it?"

"Sounds good. Don't dress up, now. Just jeans or something comfortable," he told her, starting toward the door.

"Fine. And, Logan—"

"Hm?" He turned back to her.

"Do you have any fat puppies? I like 'em fat. And a boy—I want a boy, I think."

He nodded soberly. "Right. A fat boy puppy. I'll check that out just as soon as I get home," he promised with a wondering shake of his head.

11

This was still another side of Logan, Danni decided, watching him on his knees beside the lovely, mahogany setter and her frisky babies. Looking comfortable and relaxed in his old jeans and plaid flannel shirt, he picked up one squirming, copper-colored puppy after another for Danni's inspection, grinning over each one like a proud father.

But she continued to mull over her decision until at last Logan expelled a disgusted snort and grumbled up to the silver-haired man standing nearby, "I used to think a puppy was a puppy, didn't you, Tucker? Seems I was wrong."

Tucker smiled his understanding at Danni, and even as preoccupied as she was with the plump little bundles of warm fur at her fingertips, she was taken with the inherent kindness of the man's face.

Logan had explained as he drove her out to the farm for Thanksgiving dinner that Tucker was an ex-Dallas detective who had befriended him when he was a street cop fresh out of the academy.

"He was shot up pretty badly several years ago during a drug bust," he told her as they pulled onto the dirt road leading to his place. "Not too long after Teresa—my wife—was killed. He had to take total disability and retire, so I asked him to move out here. I didn't want to stay in town . . . in our house . . . after Teresa died, and I'd always wanted a farm, at least a small one. But I knew I couldn't take care of a place like this alone, with the hours I work, so having Tucker kind of manage things for me made it possible. It's worked out real fine for both of us." He glanced sideways at her and smiled. "You'll like him. He keeps me in line."

"I'll have to see that to believe it," Danni cracked dryly.

But half an hour with the older man had convinced her that Tucker Wells could indeed manage Logan—or anyone else. An intriguing man who looked far more like a middle-aged college professor than a former big-city detective, he had a soft Texas drawl and mannerisms that spoke of a good education and a great deal of wisdom. His slender physique and patrician features, his shining silver hair and wire-framed eyeglasses all worked together to give him a refined, almost genteel appearance even in his rough work clothes. Danni had liked him immediately.

Now, as she continued to haggle over her choice of puppies, she finally scooped up the darkest and the smallest. He wiggled and thrashed his legs fiercely, then gave her a big wet kiss on the nose.

"This one," she said firmly.

Logan frowned in surprise. "You said you wanted a fat one. That's the runt of the litter. Even though he thinks he's the boss of the bunch."

"Logan named him 'Chief' about a week after he was born," Tucker said with a chuckle. "He thinks he's real tough."

"The runt, huh?" Danni said, glancing at Logan, who was watching her and the puppy closely.

"Just like you, Half-pint," he replied.

"Nope," she countered. "I *was* the litter. An only child."

"Spoiled?"

"Is that a question or an observation?"

His slow grin was her answer.

"What about you?" she asked Logan. "And don't tell me *you* were the runt!"

Tucker laughed at their banter, but Logan's smile had disappeared by the time he got to his feet. "No," he said shortly. "I was the oldest and the biggest."

"Of how many?" Danni asked.

"Six."

"Mm. I think I envy you. I always wanted a whole houseful of brothers and sisters."

He reached out a hand to help her up from her knees without acknowledging her last remark.

"Why are you keeping the puppies here," Danni asked, glancing around the enclosed porch, "instead of in the barn?"

Still holding onto her hand, Logan led her back into the living area of the cabin. "The new barn's not quite done yet. And after the old one being torched, I wouldn't feel right about putting Sassy and the pups out there."

"*Torched*?" Danni stared up at him in astonishment. "You mean someone deliberately set fire to your barn? You didn't tell me that—you just said it burned down!"

"It did—with a little help," he said tightly. He pulled her denim jacket off the wall hook and held it for her. "C'mon, I'll show you around the rest of the place. Not that there's all that much to see," he added, "but I need to walk off Tucker's biscuits." He shrugged into his flight jacket and took her by the hand.

Danni started to go with him, then turned back to Tucker, who was standing in the doorway between the porch and the living room. "How long will I have to wait before I can take Chief home, Tucker?"

"No more than two or three weeks. I'll try to housebreak him for you in the meantime," Tucker answered with a smile.

"Give that man a medal," she declared, turning back to Logan.

He draped his arm casually about her shoulder on the way to the barn. Danni knew it was just a friendly gesture, but she couldn't quite keep her feelings impassive. She simply . . . *reacted* to the man, and there seemed to be no help for it. And it wasn't all physical, although she *was* attracted to him. No, it had much more to do with the essence of the man, his strength and gentleness, his wit and rare moments of vulnerability, his idealism that somehow softened to good-natured tolerance with Danni—everything that made him . . . Logan.

"Why would anyone want to burn down your barn?" she asked him. They were standing in the middle of the new one, Logan leaning comfortably against one of the stalls while Danni retied the laces of her tennis shoes.

"I have a couple of ideas about that." His tone was hard as he continued. "And they got more than my barn. I had a brand new Charolais bull I'd saved for for over three years. He was going to be the start of a small herd of quality beef cattle for Tucker and me." He shoved both hands deep into his pockets. "He was trapped inside the barn along with two heifers."

"Oh, Logan—I'm sorry! That's awful!"

A combination of frustration and anger crossed his features. "There wasn't anything we could do. It was late. We were both asleep. By the time we got out there, it was almost gone. Went up like a tinder box."

"Do you think you'll ever find out who did it?"

He stared down at her with a grim set to his mouth. "Oh, I'll find out," he said evenly. "Count on it." He continued to meet her gaze for a long moment until his mood lightened. "You cold, Half-pint?"

Danni nodded. "A little. I could use some more of Tucker's coffee."

"Sounds good," he agreed, pulling her to her feet, then moving back from her abruptly. He stood there, looking down at her intently, searching her face, and Danni felt as though he were trying to make some sort of decision.

They were standing very close to each other, and Danni felt her heart begin to hammer at the look in his eyes. For one crazy moment she was certain he was about to kiss her, and she wondered if she would let him, admitting to herself that she wanted him to. But he didn't, and the moment passed, leaving Danni puzzled—and unnerved. Because in that moment of closeness, she had seen an assortment of feelings ricochet across his features, each combating the other in a bid for dominance. The slow-dawning under-standing that appeared for a brief instant was quickly banished by a hint of reluctance, a fitful spark of doubt, then replaced by a pool of quiet sadness, a faint but always present grief.

When they returned to the cabin, they found a cozy fire crackling in the fireplace and a fresh pot of coffee on the stove. Tucker joined them at the harvest table, and the three of them sat around drinking coffee and stuffing themselves on the pecan pie he had made earlier in the day.

"I thought maybe your cousin—Philip—would be here this evening, too," Danni remarked to Logan.

"No, Phil never comes around. He's strictly a town boy. He thought I was crazy for buying a place way out here," he replied, his cheerful, relaxed expression quickly replaced by a dark frown. "Why? Were you hoping he'd be here?"

Surprised at the sudden sharpness in his tone, Danni swallowed quickly and said in a rush of words, "No, of course not! I just thought since you were family . . . you know . . . " She let the sentence trail off, then deliberately forced a change of subject.

"Tucker, I can't decide which I like best, your biscuits or your pie," Danni said between bites. "You're a wonderful cook!"

"Well, now, it surely is refreshing to hear a kind remark about my efforts in the kitchen for a change," Tucker answered soberly, darting a meaningful glance at Logan.

"Surely you wouldn't dare complain about his cooking," Danni chided Logan. "Why, he's an even better cook than my mother!"

"He's also going to be positively unbearable for the next ten days, thanks to that statement," Logan said with a slight twitch at one side of his mouth.

"You're entitled, Tucker," Danni told him, glancing about the rustic cabin with an admiring eye. "I really like your cabin," she said to Logan. "Was it here when you bought the farm?"

He shook his head. "No, we put it up. Tucker did most of it. He's the craftsman. I just hammer nails and paint."

Danni stared with admiration at the man sitting across from her, a quiet smile of pleasure on his face at Logan's compliment. "Well, it's really special," she said, noting with interest how the entire cabin seemed to be an extension of Logan's personality.

It was rustic, but not spartan, with a definite feeling of spaciousness. The living area and kitchen were combined to form one large room with steps leading off the kitchen to a loft. Tucker mostly had the back of the cabin to himself. The enclosed porch, where Sassy and her puppies had been temporarily installed, served as a bedroom and sitting room for him. The walls were weathered siding, and the plank floors were bare except for two or three brightly colored rag rugs. Logan mentioned that Tucker had made all the tables, which held a variety of salt-glazed jugs and baskets. Bookshelves lined one entire wall and among the books was an impressive looking stereo component system. A large, crude mantel rested over the enormous stone fireplace, and above it hung a Confederate flag, which had brought a knowing grin to Danni's face earlier. There were no curtains at the windows, only shutters which could be left open or closed. It was very much a man's home, and yet it had a warmth, a charm that appealed strongly to Danni.

Tucker excused himself to take a walk. Danni had been surprised earlier to notice how quick and deft most of his movements were in spite of the fact that his entire right side from the hip down appeared to be quite stiff and immobile. As Tucker went out the door, Danni got up from the table, too. "I should get going, Logan. I have to go in early tomorrow."

While Logan went to lock the back door, Danni put on her jacket and then walked over to a large old rolltop desk. A framed photograph sat atop it, and Danni picked it up for a closer look. A younger Logan looked out at her, a Logan with shorter hair and no beard, with his arm around a tall, lovely young woman in a white suit who was smiling up at the man next to her as though he were her very world. There was a happiness, an exuberance in his face that Danni had never seen. For just an instant, she felt an unpleasant stab of jealousy.

When she realized he'd come to stand beside her, she jumped guiltily and set the picture back in place, saying quietly, "This is Teresa?"

He nodded. "That's our wedding picture."

"She was very beautiful, Logan."

He smiled down at the picture, then at Danni, and there was a kind of wistful thoughtfulness in the smile. "I think you would have liked her. She was a real special lady."

"I'm sure she was," Danni murmured, wondering if the tight little ache at the back of her throat was because she hurt for his loneliness or because she was envious of the woman who had been able to make Logan look so happy.

They were both quiet for several minutes after they got in the jeep and started back to town. Logan seemed content to drive in silence, and Danni couldn't shake off the troubling questions that invaded her thoughts. Questions about what he was beginning to mean to her, and what, if anything, she might mean to him.

The night was silent, too, thick with darkness and fog. She was startled when she felt his hand cover hers with a gentle squeeze. "I'm glad you came tonight," he said softly, glancing over at her. "Tucker really liked you."

"He's such a nice man, Logan. And he obviously dotes on you."

He continued to hold her hand, looking back at the road, slowing down somewhat and squinting into the fog. "He means a lot to me. Actually, he's been like a father to me."

Danni was surprised, but pleased, by his uncharacteristic frankness. "What about your real father, Logan? Is he still living?"

A muscle at the corner of his mouth tightened. "No," he said flatly. "Both my parents are dead."

"I'm sorry, I didn't know," she murmured. "What about the rest of your family? You said there were six of you?"

He didn't answer right away, darting an appraising look at her. When he finally spoke, his voice was hard and emotionless. "You must know about my family—you grew up here." Without giving her time to respond, he continued in the same cold, exact tone. "The last of the old-time sharecroppers. White trash, I believe we were called when I was a kid," he said harshly, with a rough sound of derision. "My old man drank himself to death, and my mother worked herself to death."

Danni wasn't sure whether the gruffness she heard in his voice was anger or sorrow. Perhaps both. She felt the need to say something to break the tension that had seemed to rise between them with his words. "I . . . suppose I was just enough younger than you that I wouldn't remember your folks—"

He laughed coarsely. "It's not likely you'd have known my folks under any circumstances." Releasing her hand, he raked his fingers through the hair at the back of his collar.

"Logan—"

"I had four sisters and one brother," he droned on as though he didn't hear her. "My brother died in the state penitentiary a few years back. He was stabbed . . . during a riot." He drew in a deep breath before going on. "I don't see my sisters much. One took off when she was fifteen and never came back. The oldest one, Julie, stays busy changing husbands. She's living in Scottsboro right now."

"And the other two?" Danni asked quietly, sensing his need to finish what he'd started.

"They're okay," he said a little more cheerfully. "Carrie— she's the youngest—went to college for a couple of years and married a real nice guy. They live in Shreveport and have two little boys. Joanne isn't married. She's a nurse at a veterans hospital in Georgia." His hands on the steering wheel relaxed slightly, but he continued to stare straight ahead of him as though he were alone in the car.

Feeling a need to say something, Danni offered hesitantly, "I imagine everyone has some things about their family they'd just as soon forget, Logan."

He expelled a sharp sound of disgust, glancing over at her. "Danni, my *dog* has a better pedigree than I—"

The sudden sharp thump against the car brought a scream from Danni. Logan swerved and hit the brake but it was too late. A raccoon, its wild, terrified eyes reflecting the glare from the headlights, stared at them in panic, then fell, got up, and dragged itself across the pavement into the woods lining the road.

Stunned, Logan watched it, his eyes filled with horror at what he'd done. "It's hurt! You stay here, I'm going after it!" Before the words were out of his mouth, he jumped from the jeep and raced into the woods, leaving Danni to huddle alone in the cold darkness.

She knew when she saw him coming out of the thick grove of trees that he hadn't been able to find the raccoon. His walk was heavy, and there was a strained, distressed look in his eyes when he slid in under the steering wheel.

He shook his head, saying nothing for a moment, then leaned wearily against the seat, closing his eyes and rubbing both hands down either side of his face. "I couldn't find him," he said with a heavy sigh. "He's either hurt bad and crawled off somewhere to die—or he wasn't hurt that much at all and went on home to dinner."

"I'm sure he's all right," Danni reassured him. "And, Logan—it wasn't your fault. You didn't mean to hit him, after all."

"It *was* my fault," he said flatly. "If I'd had my eyes on the road where they belonged, it wouldn't have happened."

"Don't be so hard on yourself," Danni ventured quietly.

He opened his eyes and, still leaning heavily against the seat, turned and looked at her.

"Well, you are, you know," she murmured awkwardly. "You expect too much from people, Logan—including yourself."

"Are you charging for this counseling session, Half-pint, or is it on the house?" he questioned softly, his eyes glinting with just a trace of amusement.

Suddenly, for some inexplicable reason, Danni wanted to touch him—right now, while he still had that soft, vulnerable expression on his face, before he could replace it with the hard-as-nails mask he usually wore. She did reach out her hand to him, halting just before her fingers would have brushed against him.

"You're a fake, Logan McGarey," she said quietly, her voice thickened by a touch of wonder, as though she had just made an important discovery.

He looked at her, soberly and expectantly, then covered her hand with his own much larger one, looking down at the small, slender fingers in his grasp as though he couldn't quite decide what to make of them. With a slow, deliberate movement, he raised her hand and placed it against the side of his face, holding it there, pressed gently against his bearded cheek.

"And what does that mean?" he questioned, a one-sided smile touching his lips.

Danni stared at her hand, marveling at the softness of the thick sable beard at her fingertips. Something in her throat swelled tightly, and she fought to keep her voice from crumbling. "You know exactly what I mean. You have everyone thinking you're such a tough guy."

His smile grew, became indulgent and just a little teasing. "Are you telling me I've blown my cover?"

She nodded, trying hard to swallow against the enormous knot in her throat. Suddenly she couldn't look into those midnight eyes any longer and glanced quickly away into the thick, silent darkness crowding in about them. "If you want to know that I think, I think you're about as hardhearted as a lump of peanut butter."

"Is that right?" he asked quietly an instant before she felt him move toward her. "Well, now, if you know me that well, then you also know I haven't entirely leveled with you about something else."

The question Danni had been about to ask died in her throat when she turned back to him. She saw something in his eyes that hadn't been there before . . . something soft and tender and infinitely caring.

His eyes never left hers as he slowly moved her hand from his face to rest on his shoulder, then gathered her into the warm circle of his arms. He was still smiling, his lips now just a breath away from her own. "I've been trying to convince both of us," he whispered, "that you're nothing more than a sharp little thorn in my side." His last few words were almost lost as he murmured them against the side of her mouth.

"But the truth is, sweet Danni, that you've become a lot more like a soft little ache in my heart."

And then he kissed her, and suddenly it didn't seem to be night anymore. There wasn't any darkness outside the car or in . . . just the faint light in Logan's eyes and the warm, steady glow reaching out from her heart to his. Danni had never been kissed that way before, not by anyone. There was a sweetness in Logan's embrace, the touch of his lips on hers, that made her feel as though she were the most special, cherished gift in the whole world. She was sure he could hear her heart hammering. In her ears, at least, it sounded as though it were going to explode any moment.

When he finally moved his hands to her shoulders to put her gently from him, a whole collage of emotions seemed to spray across his features. Danni thought she saw reluctance when he drew away from her. She knew she saw a glimmer of surprise.

She could feel his hands trembling upon her shoulders. She searched his eyes, wanting desperately to understand what she saw there, yet almost frightened by the intensity of emotion shining out from him.

"What are you doing to my life, sweetheart?" he asked softly, his gaze burning into hers. "I haven't been quite right since that night I saw you standing in a puddle at Ferguson's, lookin' like a sad-eyed kitten just washed up on the creekbank."

"You surely do have a way with words, Logan," Danni mumbled, barely breathing, shivering as he very gently tucked a strand of light hair behind her ear.

His smile was tender but uncertain. "Danni . . . I told you what I did about my family because I wanted you to hear it from me. So you'd know exactly where I come from, what I am." His expression sobered even more, as he said firmly, "I don't want any secrets between us."

Danni felt a wave of guilt wash over her. She knew he suspected her, at the very least, of being evasive with him.

But as much as she hated it, for now she would have to keep her secrets. Unable to meet his searching gaze, she turned her face away. "Why is that, Logan?" she asked in a small voice.

With one finger, he lifted her chin and forced her to look at him. "When a man is dead set on makin' a perfect fool of himself over a lady, the least he can do is be honest, don't you think?"

Wide-eyed, Danni stared at him, trying to halt the sudden riot of her feelings, but instead going numb at the sweetness of his smile, the gentle warmth in his eyes. "I—I don't understand."

He kissed her lightly on the cheek just once. "Ah, Danni, you will . . . believe me, you will." His finger touched her cheek where he'd just kissed her, and his smile slowly faded as his eyes searched hers. "I don't s'pose you'd go along with me locking you up in one of my cells for safekeeping, would you?"

"What—"

His expression grew even more serious as his fingers combed gently through her soft hair. "You scare me," he murmured, his eyes boring into hers as though he were trying to read her thoughts. "There's something—elusive—about you. I can't shake the feeling that you may disappear into the fog one of these nights unless I hold onto you."

Suddenly, almost fiercely, he pulled her back into his arms. His large hand coaxed her head against his chest, his words nearly lost as he pressed his lips into the gentle fragrance of her hair. "What am I afraid of, Danni? Why do I think I have to hold on real tight so you won't slip away from me?"

Not answering, Danni shut her eyes tightly and gave herself up, just for the moment, to the secure warmth of his strength, the sweet haven of his arms. *Oh, Logan, I hope you mean that . . . I hope you will hold on tight, because I don't want to slip away from you . . . I'm scared too, Logan . . . really scared . . . .*

12

Danni slowly straightened from crouching beside her desk in an attempt to retrieve the earring she'd dropped, moaning at the stiffness in her back and the angry rebellion of a number of other muscles. She wondered how many more karate lessons it would take before she no longer felt like the victim of a mugging after each one. Of course, last night had been only her second session, but she had exercised fiercely during the week between the two classes, hoping it would help to alleviate at least a part of the pain.

So much for that theory, she thought, moving to her office window. She raised her arms in a deep—and uncomfortable—stretch.

As she stood there, staring out with no real interest at the overcast December day, she felt the glow from the few minutes spent with Logan after class last night still hovering about her heart. They had been together every evening since Thanksgiving, even when his work schedule made more than a brief hour or two impossible. As he had walked her to her car after last night's class, he'd informed her that he had the coming weekend free and wanted to take her to Scottsboro for dinner on Saturday evening. "We need some unhurried time to talk," he'd said, searching her eyes with a questioning intensity before brushing his lips lightly over her forehead.

She hugged her arms tightly against her, smiling at the anticipation she felt just wondering what he wanted to talk about. But her sense of well-being was rudely shattered by the reminder that Logan's interest in her would most likely take a sudden tumble once he learned that she'd been deceiving him from the very beginning of their relationship.

Her reverie was suddenly broken when she caught a glimpse of movement at the infirmary. Pressing her face closer to the window, she saw Dr. Sutherland and an orderly exit the building with two elderly women between them.

The doctor was a member of the Colony who lived in the dormitories. To Danni's knowledge, he never left the premises, at least during the day. He was one of those men who, for no identifiable reason, gave Danni the creeps. He was young, plump, smooth-skinned, and looked harmless enough. But Danni had seen something in the hazel eyes behind the pop-bottle glasses that made her skin crawl. It was an expression—or lack of expression—that never failed to remind her of a documentary she'd once watched in horror about a concentration camp commandant who had cold-bloodedly murdered hundreds of "political prisoners" after performing a number of hideous experiments upon them. Without exception, the prisoners he victimized were physically helpless—very young children or severely handicapped adults.

She followed the quartet's advance up the walk to the main building, puzzled and disturbed by the strange parade. The scene was familiar, and she knew why. The women were walking with that same lifeless, undirected shuffle that had characterized the elderly men she had seen a few nights before. Sutherland and the orderly appeared to be escorting them, but something in their posture and gait made Danni think their assistance was more physical than it seemed to be.

There was something not quite right about that infirmary. It was nothing Danni could isolate, but her reporter's instincts told her that whatever was going on with these elderly "guests" was questionable, at the very least. An uncomfortable twinge of guilt accompanied the thought that she should confide in Logan about what she'd seen the other night and again this afternoon. But he was so convinced that everyone at the Colony was up to their necks in some kind of illegal activity—and he was so dead-set on finding out what—that Danni was afraid he'd come charging through the doors and start making accusations, or even arrests, and destroy her chance of getting the entire story.

And that's just another reason for you to get moving, St. John. Get your story and get out of this place . . . and maybe, if you're lucky, you'll get enough to help Logan, too! Right. Starting now. It was time to take a tour of that infirmary.

It occurred to Danni later that she could have been a little more creative in her scenario, but a simple plea of a "granddaddy of a headache" accomplished just what she'd hoped for.

"I usually keep some aspirin in my purse or in my desk," she said in her very best delicate-and-defenseless-little-darlin'-drawl, rubbing her temples with both hands and allowing her eyelashes to flutter charmingly at the orderly. "But I emptied my bottle yesterday and forgot to replace it. This has just been a *terror* of a week!"

The orderly was big and burly, and Danni thought he seemed a little slow-witted. But to his credit he apparently recognized a lady in pain when he saw one, so before she could utter another pitiful moan, he had her sitting on a plastic-covered chair with two aspirin and a paper cup of water. He crossed his thick arms over his white-coated chest and beamed as though he'd just given her the first miracle cure for the common cold.

Danni gave him a wan smile. "I really do appreciate this. I'd never make it through the afternoon otherwise."

"Why don't you lie down for awhile? Plenty of empty beds," he said with a magnanimous gesture.

"Oh—that sounds wonderful! But would it be all right?"

" 'Course it would. That's what we're here for."

I wonder, Danni thought. "Well, I think I'll just do that. But only for a very few minutes."

As soon as she stretched out on the spotless, hospital-type bed, Danni began to fake a weariness she didn't feel. While the orderly stood at the sink with his back to her, emptying and refilling an assortment of tubes and bottles, Danni quietly took mental pictures of the room, hoping to assimilate as much detail as she could. It appeared to be perfectly ordinary, antiseptically clean and furnished with only the necessities. There was a large sink, several storage cabinets, two examining tables, half a dozen empty beds, a small desk, and a computer system.

Danni quickly closed her eyes and deepened her breathing, pretending to be asleep when the orderly approached her, stopping by the side of the bed. A moment later, she heard the door to the waiting room close, then the thud of the outside door shutting. She waited an instant, then very slowly opened her eyes. A quick glance around the room verified his absence. She jumped up from the bed and went quickly into the waiting room to look out the window. She could hardly believe her luck when she saw him heading toward the main structure, but reminded herself not to get too confident. People came in and out of the infirmary all the time, so she'd best act as swiftly as possible.

She stood in the middle of the room and quickly assessed her surroundings. Then she moved toward the long white table which held the computer and its peripherals. Several large storage containers of disks were neatly arranged in rows by the printer, and with a cautious glance behind her, Danni tried to open one. It was locked, and so was the one beside it, but the lid to the third container was ajar. She turned slightly so she could keep one eye on the door as she hurriedly flipped through the disks. Most of the labels appeared to indicate ordinary files, but a half dozen or so disks in the very back of the container piqued her interest. One was labeled *Kendrick*, and after a few seconds she connected the name to the elderly man who had recently died while visiting the Colony. It was marked with a strange symbol—some sort of code, she guessed—as were all of the others behind it. One of these had the name *Jennings* on the label.

Danni looked with frustration from the disk container to the waiting room door, trying to decide what to do. She didn't dare remove the disks from the infirmary. The blank computer screen was a tempting invitation. She was pretty good with computers, having used a variety of models in her work. Still, the orderly or someone else could walk in at any moment, and she had no way of knowing how long it might take her to load and access the files she wanted to see.

No, the safest thing to do would be to try to sneak in here tonight—much later tonight. She would be on the grounds late anyway, having reluctantly decided to attend the nightly faith service in the main building. She seldom stayed for these, but Reverend Ra had recently begun to hint that she would do well to show more interest in the Colony's philosophy. She couldn't afford to arouse his suspicions now, although she thought he *had* looked at her with a glint of speculation a couple of times recently. Tonight she would stay, and that would give her a perfect opportunity to go back to her office and wait until she could return unnoticed to the infirmary.

And you're just going to walk right in, I suppose? she questioned herself sarcastically. *You don't think they leave this place unlocked, do you?* Her gaze traveled quickly around the room, searching for an answer, finally coming to rest on a large narrow window by the sink. She walked over to it and glanced outside to check the distance to the ground.

Standing on tiptoe, she reached up and released the slide lock on the window. That should do it. Once inside, she could make copies of a few of the disks and load them on the system in her office or even her p.c. at home. She knew it was compatible to those used by the Colony.

Her decision made, she went back to the bed to retrieve her purse from the table beside it, expelling a long sigh of relief that she hadn't been caught. Her mind reeled, though, when she suddenly heard a door slam shut, followed by voices in the waiting room.

Danni took a deep breath and squared her shoulders. After waiting only a moment, she whipped the strap of her purse over her shoulder and moved to the door of the waiting room. Faking a large yawn as she walked into the room, she was caught offguard by the sight of Philip Rider standing close to the outside door, deep in conversation with the orderly who had given her the aspirin. The sight of his uniform made her momentarily think of Logan, and she wondered if Rider was a part of his cousin's campaign to drive the Colony of the Lotus out of the county.

The deputy looked even more surprised to see Danni than she did him, but his greeting flowed smoothly as he removed his uniform hat and nodded to her. "Miss St. John—Danni— I hope your being here doesn't mean you're ill."

"Oh, no—that is, not now," Danni fumbled for a graceful recovery. "I was taking advantage of one of the empty beds to sleep off a headache."

His dark gray eyes scrutinized her face. "You're not coming down with the flu, I hope. Lot of it around right now."

"No, I'm fine. I think I've just overdone it a bit, actually."

"Ah, that cousin of mine is going to have to get you in earlier at night."

Danni had the uncomfortable feeling that his remark was

calculated to let her know he was aware she and Logan had been together the night before. She ignored his comment but wondered how he *did* know. Had Logan discussed her with him? Somehow she found that unlikely. She couldn't imagine Logan discussing his personal life with anyone. "Well, I really have to get back to work," she said, not meeting his gaze. "It was nice seeing you again."

He moved quickly to take her by the arm and accompany her to the door. "I'll walk you back to your office. I've been wanting to see you anyway, but Logan keeps upstaging me."

Why did she find him so disturbing? There seemed to be no concrete reason for being annoyed by the man, and yet she was. He was always very polite, very pleasant. Very smooth. Too smooth, perhaps—was that what bothered her?

"Is there a problem?" she asked him as they started toward the *Standard* building.

"Problem?" He replaced his hat at its former jaunty angle.

"Why you're here. At the Colony."

"Oh—no. Well, no more than usual," he corrected. "I'm just following up on some things Logan's been working on." He grinned down at her. "You probably know by now that he . . . takes his job very seriously—especially in matters involving the Colony."

Even his voice was silky, Danni thought irritably. She stole a glance at him, noting again that his dark gray eyes were fringed by lashes any woman would envy, and his full, pouty mouth gave him an appealing, little-boy look that had probably melted more than a few hearts.

She breathed a silent sigh, deciding that she must have a real problem when a man like this one had the same effect on her as long fingernails being raked across a blackboard. A brief, tantalizing image of a darker man, less handsome perhaps but far more endearing, brought a sweet touch of gladness to her heart. *The real problem, St. John,* she scolded herself, *is not Philip Rider at all. And you've known that for some time now, haven't you?*

Her wandering attention returned when she realized he had apparently asked her a question and was waiting for an answer. "I'm sorry—what?"

Danni thought his smile might have been somewhat strained. "I asked how you like your job by now."

"Oh, I enjoy it! They keep me busy, but it's all very interesting."

"Logan hasn't convinced you that you're living in sin, working for them?"

His question and the edge of sarcasm in his tone angered her, and she deliberately said nothing, relieved when they reached the entrance to the newspaper building.

Touching her arm lightly, he gave her an apologetic smile. "I'm sorry—I had no right to ask that." But Danni saw no real sincerity in his eyes.

"I'm just concerned, Miss St. John—may I call you Danni? Logan sometimes carries his vendetta with the Colony too far. He means well, and I'm not saying he doesn't have reason to be suspicious of a few things." He frowned and looked away from her, out over the grounds of the Colony, before continuing. "What worries me is that it's become an obsession with him."

He was still serious when he turned back to her. "What I'm trying to say is that I hope you won't let his feelings affect your job. You apparently like what you do, and it would seem to be a very impressive position for someone as young as you are." He flashed a winning smile and then went on. "You must have some dynamite credentials."

Danni stared at him, wondering exactly what he was getting at. "I'm probably not as young as you think. And I *have* had a fair share of experience."

"You're a very intriguing lady," he said softly, giving her a

121

speculative look from his heavy-lidded eyes. "And I would still like very much to take you to dinner. Is that ever going to happen?"

Danni was careful not to show her real feelings when she replied. "Not in the near future, I'm afraid. For the next few weeks, I'm probably going to be working most evenings."

"Well, I'm a patient man. I'll just keep trying until we work it out." He touched his hat lightly and added before walking away, "Have a nice evening now."

Danni stared after him for a moment, noticing that he returned to the infirmary rather than going to his patrol car.

13

It was always the same, Danni thought, slipping in between Add and Sister Lann. She made herself as comfortable as possible as she squatted Indian-fashion on the floor with the others who were awaiting the entrance of Reverend Ra and his assistants. However, there was one difference tonight. At the last service she'd attended two weeks ago, she'd seen only about a dozen elderly "visitors" among the students. Tonight she was surprised to find three times that many. Where had they all come from in such a short time—and what exactly were they doing here?

As she had at the last service, Danni turned her attention away from the room for a moment and silently prayed that the Lord would forgive her, like Naaman, for having even a small part in this. She found it difficult to endure the faith services, feeling them to be a mockery of everything these young people needed to know. But she had never won a worthwhile expose the easy way.

She found no problem in allowing Danni St. John to appear to be comfortably traditional, slightly helpless, and even a bit of a fluffhead. Indeed, it was a fairly easy role since, if she were to be brutally truthful about herself, she would have to admit that she was hopelessly unorganized, unscheduled, and unmethodical.

On the other hand, the heart of D. Stuart James burned with an unquenchable fire to remove the protective veil from the growing number of criminals in high places who victimized the helpless and the hopeless, and to bring to their collective knees those unprincipled charlatans who made their fortunes by feeding on the lonely, searching hearts of hurting people.

It was D. Stuart James who had worked six months as a ward secretary in a successful northeastern clinic to help put behind bars the two physician-partners who had grown phenomenally wealthy through their slick, nearly infallible operation wherein healthy organs were obtained illegally and then sold via a blackmarket syndicate at astronomical prices to desperate recipients.

It was D. Stuart James who had put her own life on the line by posing as the distraught wife of another freelance journalist, himself a cancer patient. Accompanying him to one of the most notorious healing centers for cancer in the world, she had eventually exposed the entire, fraudulent organization.

And it was D. Stuart James who, only eighteen months ago, had spent a week in the hospital recovering from a particularly vicious assault that occurred when she was caught taking pictures of physical abuse at a day care center for the elderly while employed as an aide.

Now D. Stuart James was home and after the biggest story of her career, one especially dear to her heart. For D. Stuart James—the pen name Danni St. John used for all her undercover journalism—hated, more than any other form of deception, religious fraud.

She had researched the Colony of the Lotus for months. Then, using the considerable credentials she had obtained under her real name, she'd gone after—and won—the position as editor of the *Peace Standard*.

So, if sitting through one of Reverend Ra's phony faith services was a necessary evil, Danni told herself again, sit through it she would. She knew full well that it might not be the worst of what she would have to endure before she got what she needed for her story. And as she watched the young people all around her bending over to touch their foreheads to the floor, chanting the usual meaningless nonsense, she wondered if that story might not be a great deal bigger than what she'd originally suspected.

She folded her hands and tried to appear interested while they repeated their Sacred Promise to the Master Guide. Reverend Ra had entered and now stood at their center. His arms were upraised and his eyes closed as he softly voiced a number of affirmations to the words being sent up around him. He was an impressive sight, Danni had to give him that. The white flowing robe and the shining silver stole that almost perfectly matched his hair made the man a tall, shimmering spire in the midst of the chanting young people.

When they began their communal chant, Danni shuddered. She kept her eyes closed and prayed fiercely for the binding of any evil presence from the room. She especially disliked this particular part of the service, for she felt the chanting itself was a kind of hypnotic, mind-numbing experience for those taking part in it.

Not that these kids needed anything else to deaden their brains, she thought resentfully. Without a doubt, Logan had been right on target when he'd accused the Colony of being heavily into drug abuse.

She wondered if anyone, other than the leaders, was aware of the association of the Colony's name with the drug culture. The ancient Greeks had believed that the fruit of the Lotus plant caused a dreamlike state, enabling one to leave reality, eventually destroying all desire to ever return home. In the legends, the "Lotus Eaters" became so dependent on it and its resulting indolency that they never sought reality again. She felt certain that was happening to most of the members of the Colony.

Including Add, she thought sadly, opening her eyes to glance at the youth sitting beside her. Although he often seemed torn and confused, occasionally reacting to some comment of Danni's about her own faith or a particular attribute of the Lord, more and more lately he seemed to be slipping away into that misty, inaccessible place where the other students existed. The thought made her ill. The boy had such promise. He had the soul of an artist and a highly gifted mind. *And if there's any way to get him out of this place,* she suddenly thought with determination, *I'm going to do it!*

When the service ended, Danni started to get to her feet, but Reverend Ra put out a restraining hand and asked everyone to wait. At that point, he called off a dozen or so names from a list handed to him by Brother Penn.

"Each of you has been assigned a city to visit. You will go out among the people who need to live again and bring them to us. Just as we have provided shelter for others in need," he gestured toward the group of elderly men and women sitting to his left, "so will we offer a haven for all who would enter to find peace in our midst."

Danni breathed a deep sigh of relief when Add's name wasn't one of those called. "How do the students go about making contact with prospective guests?" she asked him as they filed out of the communal room.

"I've never been a guide," he said, waiting for her to exit the room ahead of him. "I've always worked within the family. But I think they go to the places where people in trouble can usually be found. You know, the hospital charity wards, mission centers, bus stations. There are many who need us in those places."

"But why? I mean, why do it in the first place?"

He stared at her as though she were the adolescent and he the adult. "They need help," he answered simply.

"And they're willing to leave? To get on a bus and come here with strangers?"

He shrugged. "We have much more to offer them than what they already have. Why wouldn't they come?"

"What, Add? What exactly *is* offered to these people?"

He glanced around, but no one was nearby. Everyone was

126

making their way to the dormitories, and Reverend Ra was talking with Dr. Sutherland. "Well—a lot," he said evasively. "You know, shelter, food, people who care—we meet their needs."

"How can the Colony afford to do that for so many?"

He looked at her blankly for a long moment. "I don't know. It's all taken from the family bank, I suppose."

"The family bank?"

He nodded. "Whatever we have, we give to the family when we come here and it's kept in trust for all of us."

"You mean you have no money of your own—none at all?"

He gave her a puzzled smile. "Why would we need money? The Master Guide gives us everything we need."

Danni studied his young, wholesome features, searching his glazed eyes for a long time. "Yes," she replied softly. "I'm sure he does."

She paused at the outside door. "Well, I'll see you tomorrow, Add. I'm going back to the office for awhile."

"Want me to go with you, Miss St. John?"

"No, no—I'm just going to tie up some loose ends. It'll only take a few minutes."

The smooth voice at her back startled her, and she whirled around abruptly. "Well, Sister, it's good to see you among us tonight. I've been hoping our editor would show a bit more interest in the family." Reverend Ra was beaming down at her with what was supposed to be, Danni assumed, fatherly approval.

Danni moved her glasses down from the top of her head to her nose. "Yes. Well, it's all very . . . interesting to me. Different, of course. But interesting."

His smile appeared to be glued into place. "If you have questions about our philosophy or our work, Sister, please remember that I'm available to you at any time. I'll be only too happy to share and instruct you when I can."

Danni felt almost as though he were physically drawing her into his sinister blue eyes. She had to steel herself against backing away from him as she mumbled, "Thank you. I appreciate that."

"We haven't seen nearly enough of you, Sister. I hope we haven't placed too heavy a workload upon those small shoulders of yours." He reached out a large, heavy hand to touch her on the shoulder.

Something in his gaze had changed, and Danni was hit like a bolt of lightning by the thought that the sanctimonious Reverend Ra was devouring her with his eyes like a greedy man faced with a new menu. Her mouth went suddenly dry. This time she did move away from him.

"Not at all," she rasped, then cleared her throat and added, "I confess to being somewhat of a workaholic. I enjoy being busy."

"Admirable," he said, removing his hand but not his gaze. "However, we want you to have time for spiritual growth as well. Please plan to join us more often."

Danni almost gagged, glaring at him as he walked away. *Spiritual growth indeed!*

It was ten-thirty. Danni had stayed in her office, pretending to work, until it was unlikely that anyone would be wandering about the grounds.

A cold dampness and heavy fog filled the night, giving it a clammy, oppressive stillness. Danni pressed herself against the end wall of the infirmary, leaning against it for a long time, listening but hearing nothing as she forced herself to take deep, even breaths.

Finally, taking one long breath of chilled air, she hoisted herself up on one of the garbage pails she'd tugged into place. With a careful glance around her, she began to slowly raise the window she'd left unlocked. It didn't give easily; she had to brace one knee on the window sill and push upward as hard as possible, almost losing her balance in the effort. But the last push did it. Quickly she swung over the sill and dropped lightly inside the dark examining room. For one of the few times in her life, she was grateful for being a "Half-pint," as her dad—and lately Logan—had dubbed her.

Standing very still, hardly breathing, she tried to decide whether she should leave the window open or close it. If someone happened by, an open window would be a dead giveaway. On the other hand, what if she had to get out in a hurry? She decided to take her chances with the open window.

She took a few cautious steps away from the wall. The only light in the room was a dim glow from the outside security light a few feet from the building, so she dug down into her skirt pocket for the small penlight she'd brought along, flashing its narrow beam in front of her.

Tiptoeing stealthily to the doorway of the waiting room, she peeked inside. Seeing nothing, she turned back to the examining room and made her way quietly to the computer.

With trembling fingers she turned on the computer and booted up the system disk in the left drive. While it was loading, she went to the disk container that had been unlocked earlier, praying it would be open. It was—and so was the one beside it.

Her hands were shaking so badly she could hardly separate the disks. She finally managed to pull three of them from their envelopes. Inserting one into the right drive, she called up the index. Every file appearing on the monitor was coded with some sort of number and letter that reminded Danni of chemistry symbols she'd long ago forgotten. Pulling half a dozen blank diskettes from her purse, she began to systematically copy some of the disks from the container.

It was tricky, trying to feed disks into the system in a dark room with palms so sweaty she could barely hold on to the penlight. The longer she stood there, swallowing against the lump in her throat every time her gaze flicked over the open window, the more panicky she became. One more disk and she'd be done. *Please, Lord, just one more* . . . .

She jumped, then froze, almost dropping the penlight and the disk in her hand when she heard voices. They sounded as though they were directly outside the window. Forcing herself to inch over and peer out, she discovered, with only a little relief, that the two people engaged in conversation were actually passing by the infirmary. It was Brother Penn and an elderly man she'd never seen before. As a Hawk—the highest rank of students—Penn was allowed on the grounds later than those in the lesser ranks. But where were they headed?

Holding her breath, Danni strained to hear the conversation, but couldn't. It sounded as though Penn were speaking in a soothing tone to the man who appeared to be allowing himself to be led down the walkway.

Danni's relief when they didn't slow as they passed by was almost tangible. *Out—get out of here—now!* She hurried back to the computer table; released the last disk she'd copied; replaced the masters in the container, and turned off the system's power.

With her heart still in her throat, she carefully edged to the side of the window. Glancing around the outside area as thoroughly as possible, she crawled out of the window to stand on the unstable pail while she forced the stubborn window closed and headed toward the parking lot. She didn't slow her brisk pace until she was safely inside her car with the doors locked.

Thanks, Lord, she breathed fervently, turning the key in the ignition. Relief draped itself around her like a soft, warm blanket, and her eyes stung with hot tears. Wiping her wet cheek with the back of one hand, she turned the car onto the dirt road leading away from the Colony. A fleeting, disturbing image of the beating she'd received when her cover was blown at the day care center insinuated itself into her silent prayer, but she forcefully pushed it aside.

"You never said it would be easy, Father," she voiced aloud. "But you did say you'd never fail me . . . and you never have. I want to get these people, Lord. I'm not sure yet just exactly what's going on behind those whitewashed walls, but with your help I'm going to find out. Just don't let fear get the best of me, please, Lord."

"The Lord is on my side; I will not fear . . . " She continued to murmur the reassuring verse of Scripture all the way home until she was safely inside her own front door.

14

Danni had to see Logan. She'd stayed up half the night loading files into her home computer, attempting to read them, printing out those she thought might have significance to her story. But for the most part, she knew little more than she had when she started.

The disks marked *Kendrick* and *Jennings* contained the only files she could make much sense of, and that was limited. But she was able to figure out that each disk was the equivalent of a personal file containing a variety of information about both dead men. A succession of dates on each disk seemed to indicate receipts and deposits of checks in a number of bank accounts. In addition, results of what appeared to be detailed investigations of each man were summarized with the conclusion that William Kendrick had no known living relatives who could be contacted. Robert Jennings, however, had been a widower survived by a sister and two married daughters. A note to the effect that his current address at the Colony was being kept confidential upon his request had been entered into his file.

At two o'clock in the morning, Danni gave up trying to decipher the mysterious symbols and numbers on the other disk files. Her brain was numb, and when she could finally keep her eyes open no longer, she admitted defeat and went to bed. Her last thought was that she would call Logan first thing when she got up and make arrangements to meet him and divulge the contents of the disks. Hopefully, he'd be able to help her make some sense of them. In doing so she'd have to reveal the truth about herself, but it was time for that. In fact, she was almost relieved that something had forced her hand. She hated deceiving him, especially in light of her feelings for him that seemed to be growing stronger and stronger.

But when she called the farm at seven-thirty the next morning, Tucker told her that Logan had already left for town. "Oh—I'm sorry I bothered you, Tucker. I didn't think he'd be gone already."

"Well, he usually wouldn't be," Tucker said in his soft, slightly nasal drawl. "But he thought he should get to the office as soon as possible this—" His voice died away and Danni heard him draw a deep breath before he continued. "You've seen the morning paper, haven't you?"

"The *Herald*? No, not yet. Why?"

His tone dropped even more in volume. "Best you read it for yourself, I think," he answered quietly. "Maybe you'll want to call him then."

"But, Tucker, what . . . " Danni set her coffee cup on the counter and started toward the kitchen table, where the morning *Herald* was still rolled up in a rubber band. When the telephone cord wouldn't reach, she gave Tucker a hasty goodbye and hung up. Grabbing the newspaper from the table, she flipped it open.

Shock ricocheted through her when she saw the enormous, bold headline: *Sheriff Accused of Brutality by Colony Student and Guest.* Her eyes widened in horrified disbelief as she scanned the article. It was a two-column-plus spread, but the essence of it was that Brother Penn and a man named Albert Weston had allegedly been detained by Logan at the county jail the evening before for "routine questioning." The charge had been made that the sheriff had "verbally harassed and humiliated them, and then proceeded to physically assault each of them, using potentially dangerous martial arts techniques." Both Penn and Weston had supposedly exhibited a number of bruises and lacerations at the time they filed charges against Logan.

Almost as bad as the screaming headline about the brutality charges was the sly, unnecessary reference to Logan's family. The fact that Logan's brother had died in prison during a riot was a prominent part of the article, coupled with a comment about one of his sisters disappearing during the time Logan was "earning medals in the Vietnam conflict." This was yellow journalism at its worst, and Danni was outraged. What made it even more painful to her was the memory of the hurt she'd sensed in Logan when he'd told her about his family. This article would be like pouring salt on an open wound.

Hurling the paper to the floor, she tore out of the kitchen and raced upstairs to change from her robe to a pair of corduroy pants and a bulky sweater. By the time she dashed out into the driveway to start her car, her throat was on fire, burning with a mixture of fury and apprehension.

Albert Weston had to be the man she'd seen walking by the infirmary with Penn last night. It had been dark, of course, but she had seen both of them clearly under the security light. She was certain neither of them had had a bruise or a cut anywhere in sight! It was a vicious lie! But even if she hadn't seen the two men, she knew Logan well enough to know he'd never abuse his karate skill in such a way! It was a deliberate attempt to discredit him.

It didn't take too much to figure out what they hoped to accomplish. If there was any way they could defeat Logan in the upcoming election, they'd do it. It was only a few weeks away now, and he was a definite threat to them. It could only be to their advantage to get him out of office.

Well, they aren't going to get away with it! Danni thought heatedly as she gunned the motor and screeched out of her driveway. The article said they'd been released at nine-thirty, over an hour before she'd seen them back at the Colony. *I can prove there wasn't a mark on those two when they walked by the infirmary.*

Then it hit her. She couldn't prove anything of the kind, not without revealing her own whereabouts at the time. How, exactly, could she explain being inside the locked infirmary an hour and a half after she had supposedly left the faith service?

The realization of the trap she was in hit her with a sick thud in the stomach. In order to clear Logan, she would have to blow her own cover. That would mean the loss of months of research and time as well as the loss of a story she considered vital to young people all over the country. In addition, she'd lose the chance to prove another suspicion that had been growing stronger each day she was at the Colony—that there was something more evil going on than she'd first thought. Something that had to do with the elderly "visitors" the Colony was housing in ever increasing numbers.

But how could she *not* tell what she knew? To keep quiet was to play right into their hands. They'd get away with smearing Logan and casting doubt on his integrity as sheriff. And he was a *good* sheriff. In fact, Danni thought worriedly, Logan McGarey might well be the last, best hope of the entire town of Red Oak. With Logan out of the picture, it would only be a matter of time before the entire area belonged to the Colony of the Lotus.

Her decision was made. She had to tell Logan the truth, all of it. And she would tell the authorities what she had seen the night before, if that's what it would take to clear Logan of this ridiculous charge. If it meant losing her job as editor before she could wrap up the story, then so be it. There was no way she could keep all this under wraps any longer. There was too much at stake for him and for the town. If the truth would help Logan, then he would have it. Today.

She stuck her head inside the doorway of the office

waiting room, but saw no one. When she entered, she could hear Logan talking with someone, then decided after a moment he must be on the phone. Danni sat down on an uncomfortable wooden chair and picked up a magazine which was over a year old. She leafed through it randomly, then put it down and rose from her chair when she no longer heard Logan talking.

He looked up from his desk, then quickly pushed his chair back and stood when he saw her in the office doorway. Something tugged at Danni's heart when she saw the shadows under his dark eyes. His uniform, at any other time immaculate and perfectly pressed, was rumpled. He looked tired, worried, and much older than his thirty-three years. But his smile was warm with apparent pleasure at the sight of her.

"Hello," he said quietly, not moving from behind the desk but searching her eyes as if he were trying to read her thoughts.

She walked the rest of the way into his office, not quite knowing what to say, then blurted out, "I saw the paper."

After a moment, he nodded, then lifted his eyebrows and attempted another smile. "You and everyone else in town."

"They can't get away with it." When he didn't answer, she pressed. "Can they?"

His shoulders drooped for only an instant before he straightened and walked around the desk to her. "Then you don't believe it?" he asked softly with a look of relief.

She stared up at him, losing her breath when she encountered the depth of feeling in his eyes. "Of course I don't believe it, Logan! Even if I hadn't—"

He waited, a puzzled frown grooving his forehead. "If you hadn't what?"

Impulsively, Danni reached out to touch him on the forearm, and when she did he covered her hand with his and

136

held onto her. "Logan, there's so much I have to tell you. We have to talk . . . . "

"What's wrong? Here, sit down." He started to lead her away from the desk.

"Maybe we should go somewhere . . . . "

They both jumped when they heard the waiting room door slam shut, followed by Philip Rider's cheerful, booming voice. He started talking before he ever reached Logan's office. "Well, Cousin, you've done it this time! Logan, couldn't you keep that temper of yours under—" He stopped halfway through the door, giving both Logan and Danni a look of extreme interest. "Sorry," he drawled with heavy emphasis. "I'll come back later." He flashed a mocking smile, then turned to leave.

"That's not necessary," Danni told him firmly. "I was just leaving." She turned back to Logan, who was staring at her with a question in his eyes.

Quickly, Danni darted a warning glance at him, hoping he wouldn't say anything else. "I'll . . . see you later this evening then?"

For a moment he looked at her blankly, then recovered. "Right. I'll be over—oh, about seven?"

"Fine. Nice seeing you again, Deputy Rider," she said evenly on her way out of the office, but she could feel his gaze on her until she was out of sight.

15

Danni left the Colony early that afternoon, explaining to Add that she had things to do at home. Actually, she spent the time remaining before Logan was due to arrive making an extra printout of everything on the disks so she could give him a copy. She finished just in time to shower and change into a pair of soft wool slacks and an oversize yellow polo shirt before the doorbell rang.

Still in uniform, he removed his leather jacket and service revolver, leaving them in the hallway closet. "Sorry about the way I look," he said, gesturing to his rumpled shirt, "but I just haven't had time to change.

"So what's wrong?" he asked bluntly, giving her an affectionate hug and planting a light kiss on top of her head as naturally as if he did it every day.

Flustered by his closeness and tense to the point of despair about her anticipated confession, Danni caught an uneven breath. She started to pull away from him as she answered in a shaky voice, "I'm hoping you can help me figure that out."

His smile was tired but tender as he stared down into her eyes, deliberately holding onto her so she couldn't move away from him.

"Logan—"

"Let me just hold you for a minute, okay?"

His need to draw strength from her enfolded Danni like a sweet caress. She willingly rested her head against his chest, standing quietly in his arms, neither of them saying a word. Her stomach tightened as she wondered how quick he would be to touch her once he knew the truth.

Reluctantly, she eased out of his embrace and glanced up at him with concern, seeing the faint lines of fatigue webbing out from his eyes and around his mouth.

"What kind of reaction have you had so far—to the newspaper article?" she asked.

He shrugged. "Mixed. Mostly calls from people who think I'm a real bad guy." He tried to smile. "Goes with the turf, I s'pose."

"Have you had anything to eat? Dinner?"

"Not yet," he admitted. "But I wasn't expecting you to feed me. I thought we'd go out—unless you don't want to be seen with the strong arm of the law."

"Don't be ridiculous. But I'd rather stay here, where we can talk. I have some ham and leftover roast beef, if you don't mind cold cuts."

"No buttermilk, I s'pose?"

"As a matter of fact," she said smugly, "I have a half-gallon. Fresh from the grocery today."

He grinned with extreme pleasure. "I think I'm in love," he drawled, pulling her by the hand toward the kitchen.

Danni knew he was joking, but her heart felt as though it were tumbling over in her throat at his words. "Tell me about last night," she said as they began unloading the refrigerator.

Logan rolled up his shirt sleeves and started to slice off some roast beef while Danni fixed a platter of ham and cheese.

He shrugged, wielding the knife like a machete. "I went over to the bus station to pick up a package that was supposed to come in on the bus from Chattanooga. I saw Penn and Weston at the ticket counter." He put the knife in the sink and carried the plate of roast beef over to the table. "What else do you want me to do?"

"That's all. Sit down, and we'll eat."

He held Danni's chair for her and scooted in close beside her, waiting while she offered a prayer of thanks.

"So—go on," Danni prompted as they filled their plates.

"Well, they were arguing," he explained, spearing a pickle. "The old man, especially, seemed upset. I tried asking them a few questions, and Weston said he just wanted to leave, but that Penn wouldn't let him go. Penn said he was trying to keep the old man from hurting himself, that he was sick and didn't have any business being out of bed. Then Weston started crying and grabbing on to me as though he were scared to death of something. So I put them both in the patrol car and took them down to my office to try to figure out what was going on."

"Then you didn't actually arrest them?"

"No, I never said anything about arresting them. I just told them I wanted to talk to them. It seemed to me that Weston couldn't get in the car fast enough. Penn sulked all the way downtown, but he's a little weird most of the time. Weston—well, he was all spaced out on something. He was agitated one minute and half-asleep the next."

"But you let them go—"

He nodded with a disgusted grunt, fixing himself a huge sandwich. "We hadn't been in my office any more than half an hour or so when the old man did a complete about-face. I left both of them with Phil while I went down the hall to the coffee machine to get Weston something to drink. I thought it might help to clear his head. When I came back, Weston started insisting the whole thing was all a mistake, that he wanted to go back to the Colony with Penn. So I couldn't hold them."

"But if Philip was there with you, then he knows you didn't lay a hand on them!" Danni exclaimed hopefully.

Logan took an enormous bite of his triple-decker, shaking his head at the same time. "He left before they did. A call came in from Brumleigh Road, and I sent him out there."

Disappointed, Danni left the rest of her dinner untouched. "I wonder why Mr. Weston changed his mind so suddenly?" she mused out loud. "And why would he charge you with brutality when you were only trying to help him?"

"Who knows?" he replied with a shrug. "Like I said—his head was all messed up, that was as plain as could be." With a grim look, he added, "I have to admit, I might have been tempted, just for a minute, you understand, to wipe the smirk off *Brother* Penn's face."

When Danni glanced at him with alarm, he smiled. "I said I was *tempted*, honey. I didn't lay a finger on either one of those guys."

The endearment that escaped him so easily caught Danni offguard. Quickly, she rose and began clearing the table. "I know that. What—what are you going to do?"

"There's not a whole lot I can do," he replied, getting up to help her. "The fact is that those two are walkin' around with some pretty convincing bruises and cuts on their faces. It's my word against theirs that I'm not the one who marked them up."

Standing very still, her back to him, Danni caught her lower lip beneath her teeth and held her breath. "Maybe not," she said softly.

"What?" He was peering inside the refrigerator to see what else he might find, not paying much attention to her.

"I said," Danni repeated, setting their plates in the sink, "that it's *not* just your word against theirs."

He ducked his head out of the refrigerator and closed the door, giving her a puzzled look. "What's that mean?"

With trembling hands, Danni poured coffee into tall, thick mugs.

"Danni?"

When she finally turned to face him, she met his puzzled gaze with anxious eyes, holding his mug of coffee out to him. "Let's go in the living room. I have a fire going in there."

Logan took his coffee from her, still searching her face, then reached over with his free hand and lifted Danni's steaming cup from the counter.

"Go ahead and sit down," she told him when they entered the room. "I have something I want to get." She pushed a large, dark table to the front of the couch for their coffee and left the room.

When she returned from the den with the file folders containing the printouts she'd made that afternoon, she laid them on the table and sat down beside Logan.

"What's that?"

"In a minute," she said. "Logan—about what I said in the kitchen—I can prove you didn't touch Penn or Albert Weston."

Incredulity rose in his eyes as he set his cup carefully on the table. "What are you talking about?"

Danni took a deep, steadying breath. "I saw them last night—both of them—long after they'd been in your office." She swallowed hard, desperately wishing there were some way to avoid telling him all this. It was going to cost her a great deal, but it would cost him even more if she kept quiet. "I saw them," she repeated, "but I didn't see a sign of the bruises or cuts you supposedly inflicted on them."

"I don't understand—where were you?"

"At the Colony," she supplied quickly. "They were outside the infirmary."

"The infirmary?" he repeated blankly. "What time?"

She saw what might have been relief . . . or hope . . . wash across his features when she answered. "It was after ten-thirty. Probably close to eleven o'clock."

"What in the world were you doing on the grounds that late?"

"I—wasn't exactly on the grounds," she said quietly. "I was in the infirmary."

"In the—" He raked a hand down the side of his face,

142

staring at her with bewilderment.

"I was inside the examining room . . . copying some disks."

When he started to interrupt, she held up her hand. "I heard voices and looked out," she continued. "Penn and an elderly man were walking toward the main building. I couldn't tell what they were talking about, but I could see them clearly when they got close to the security light. And they looked perfectly fine to me. No cuts or bruises." She waited only a second or two before asking, "What does Albert Weston look like?"

He thought for a moment. "He's almost bald. Big man—a lot bigger than Penn. A little overweight."

"That's the man I saw," Danni said firmly.

He blinked, his face a study in confusion. "I must have missed something here." He sat slightly forward. "Why were you copying disks in the infirmary?"

Danni avoided his gaze and reached out to open one of the files on the table in front of them. "I made a printout of what I copied. Most of it I don't understand, but maybe you will." She handed the papers from the file to him, then rose from the couch and walked over to the fireplace. After giving him a few minutes, she asked, "Does any of that makes sense to you?"

Intent on the page in front of him, he nodded. "This looks simple enough; it's some sort of personal file for William Kendrick. There's a record of bank deposits—" He broke off as he went on quickly scanning the page. "Whoa." He glanced up at Danni. "Same amount each month. Deposited in different banks. That would seem to indicate some kind of pension or government check, don't you think?"

Danni gave a small, questioning shrug. "There's another file similar to that one. For someone named Jennings."

"Jennings?" He picked up the next file and leafed through it hurriedly.

"The name means something to you?"

"He was the first 'guest' at the Colony to die. At least, the first I'm aware of." After a moment, he put the file on the table and reached for more. "That one is just like the other. It's a dossier, with a listing of bank deposits."

"Those are the ones that really have me stumped," Danni told him, gesturing to the other files he'd just picked up. "They seem to be some sort of reports—they're all numbers and coded symbols. I can't decipher any of it."

It was several minutes before he spoke. He sifted through a number of pages in two or three files, studying them intently, whistling softly in surprise once or twice. When his eyes finally met hers, Danni could see a combination of excitement and puzzlement. "They're logs. Lab journals of experiments."

Danni released a sharp breath of surprise. "What kind of experiments?"

Logan examined her face as he placed the files on the table and rose slowly from the couch, his penetrating stare holding her captive as he walked toward her. "Drug experiments," he said softly, coming to stand directly in front of her and laying both hands firmly on her shoulders. "What are you doing with this stuff, Danni? How did you get it?"

She had to tell him. There was no way to avoid it now. Still she faltered, dreading his reaction. What would he think of her, once he knew that she'd deceived him? Even though the truth could only help him, would he turn on her for misleading him all this time?

Unable to meet his eyes, Danni looked away from him, into the fire. "I told you. I copied some disks from the infirmary and did a printout on them."

"How? *Why?*" His grasp on her shoulders tightened.

Finally willing herself to look up at him, she said simply, "Let's sit down, Logan. I have something to show you . . . and something to tell you."

16

He was slow in releasing her, and when he did he moved one hand to the small of her back and followed her across the room as though he were afraid she'd get away from him. Danni stopped at a dark spinet desk and picked up a portfolio. Logan waited right behind her, moving only when she did to sit down beside her on the couch.

She unzipped the portfolio and pulled out three manila file folders and a couple of small cards, first handing Logan the files. Glancing from her to the files, he opened one of them and scanned the photocopied article on top. Darting another questioning glance at Danni, he did the same thing with the remaining files.

"I remember reading these stories," he said with a slight nod of his head and a puzzled glance at her. He laid each article out on the table, looking from one to the other again.

Danni smiled weakly when she glanced at the bold headlines, each of them carrying the same byline: D. Stuart James. She then handed Logan the two press cards she'd been holding. On one was printed the name *Danni St. John.* On the other, *D. Stuart James.*

He looked at each, turned them over once or twice, then looked blankly from the cards to Danni. "What's this?"

When she didn't answer immediately, he glanced back at the cards in his hands. Danni saw a faint spark of realization begin to dawn when he transferred his gaze from the cards to the articles lying on the table. She heard his sharp intake of breath before he ever turned to look at her. Staring fixedly at the articles, he said hoarsely, "These were . . . your stories." Then he looked at her, and Danni saw the glint of disbelief change to a spark of understanding. "Danni St. John . . . D. Stuart James. You?"

She nodded, feeling her heart thud painfully. She forced herself to meet his gaze, aching when his reddened, exhausted eyes suddenly clouded with doubt. "I don't understand," he murmured brokenly, shaking his head in bewilderment. Then he laughed roughly. "Man, is *that* an understatement!" His weak attempt at a smile faded quickly as he tossed the press cards onto the table and turned back to Danni.

There was no avoiding the hurt she saw looking out at her behind the weary, emotionally frayed expression. "So who are you *really*? What exactly is happening here?"

She moistened her lips and looked down at her hands. "I'm just . . . Danni. I use the pen name only for . . . certain kinds of stories. Exposés."

He narrowed his eyes slightly as though something had just clicked inside his mind. "Exposés?"

Danni nodded, glancing up at him. "I used it the first time I ever did any investigative reporting. It's a combination of my mother's maiden name and my father's first name. The editor I was working with at the time suggested that I might want to continue using it for similar stories."

Logan glanced over at the articles on the table. "You took some pretty wild chances, didn't you? What ever possessed you to get involved in this kind of stuff?"

Danni shrugged and gave him a wobbly grin. "Believe it or not, I believe it's what the Lord wants me to do."

When he frowned and continued staring at her, Danni felt a need to make him understand. "When I was in high school, I thought I wanted to be a missionary. I was just sure that's what I was called to do. But during my senior year, a very wise youth counselor pointed out to me that I'd made an assumption about my future without really praying for God's direction. So she spent some time with me in concentrated prayer. To make a long story short, within a few weeks God began to work in my heart to show me I wasn't being called to the mission field at all. Instead, He began guiding me to use the writing ability He'd given me." With another small, self-conscious shrug, she added, "And I suppose I've been using it ever since."

He stared at her, searching her eyes for a long time, then got up and walked over to stand gazing into the fire. When he finally turned back to her, he pushed his hands deep into his pockets and sighed heavily. "Okay. But where does this fit in with the Colony? With those files from the—" He stopped, raised his head slightly, then shook it slowly from side to side. "Oh, no. You're not that crazy." He waited, the disbelief in his expression gradually changing to reluctant insight.

"Logan—"

Anger and astonishment came together and exploded in his eyes. "*That's* what you're doing at the Colony! The job is just a front! You're after another *story!*"

"Wait a minute, Logan—"

He moved toward her, his dark eyes boiling like churning thunderclouds. "You *are* crazy! Do you have any idea what you're mixed up with here?" He was shouting at her now as he hovered over her.

"*Yes!*" she shouted back at him. "I *do!* Why else would I be here?"

Logan looked at her with a blend of fury and amazement that made Danni want to shrink back on the couch, away from him. However, what she did was to sit very still and glare up at him, refusing to let him see that his fierce tirade had her uncomfortably close to tears.

She deliberately kept her tone level, her voice tightly controlled. "It's my job, Logan. It's what I do."

"It's what you do," he growled caustically, his voice deceptively soft. "I don't suppose," he said, his tone now lowered to a threatening hiss, "it ever once occurred to you to tell me the truth from the beginning? Have you enjoyed this little masquerade, lady? Is this a new game—*Outwit Your Local Sheriff?*"

Suddenly Danni had had all she could take. The combined stress of her escapade from the night before, the fatigue of the sleepless hours she'd put in, and Logan's anger was fast draining away what little composure she had left. She jumped up from the couch and, eyes blazing, faced him. "*Stop it!* Just—*stop it!*"

He stared down into her enraged, gamin face and his anger faded to a stunned look of exasperation—as if he had suddenly forgotten what, exactly, had made him so furious.

"Correct me if I'm wrong, *Sheriff*—but I'm reasonably sure that you're the same man who lectured me not too long ago about the danger of indifference, the inherent evil of a do-nothing attitude. What was that well-known quote you ran by me recently? '*The only thing necessary for the triumph of evil is for good men to do nothing.*' Tell me, does that exclude women?"

His chin went up in a belligerent thrust, but he rested his hands on his hips in a somewhat defiant stance. "That eloquent little speech has a point somewhere, I s'pose." His voice had by now deepened to a warning rumble.

"The point," Danni grated, her usually laughing eyes now cold and impatient, "is that I'm only doing what you're always saying needs to be done. I'm putting my proverbial money where my mouth is! But for some reason that seems to set you on the warpath. I don't suppose you'd want to explain why you expect everyone else but me to have the courage of their convictions, would you? What exactly is it that exempts me from that?"

"*Because I've already seen one woman I love die! I'm not going to stand by and watch it happen all over again!*" The minute the

148

words exploded from him, the anguish that had shadowed his face only a moment before was replaced by an expression of utter amazement.

It took Danni an instant to realize that Logan's outburst had been as much of a surprise to him as it was to her. They stared at each other, the veneer suddenly stripped away, the truth finally revealed, their defenses totally down. Within seconds, there was nothing left in Logan's eyes but the finality of his admission, and nothing in Danni's but astonishment at the impact of his words. He took a step toward her and she took a step away from him.

"Logan . . ."

"Danni . . ." He stood looking down at her, his eyes filled to overflowing with what had just dawned on him as he stared at her, intensely searching for a response. They were close, so close, and Logan touched her with his eyes a long time before he took her chin gently between his thumb and forefinger to lift her face even more. "Danni—honey . . ."

The softness of his voice, the tenderness in his eyes, were her undoing. She tried to twist her lips into a smile, but it was a futile thing and quickly faded. "Well, I suppose that's a pretty good reason, after all," she said shakily.

His arms came slowly around her, pulling her into the safe haven of his strength. Wonder melted through Danni as he held her and she felt his trembling blend with her own. And then he kissed her, so gently, so softly, and with such a reverence Danni thought she'd surely never, ever feel quite so fragile or so cherished as she did at this moment.

She leaned her head against his chest, her heart swelling with a strange new kind of happiness when she heard his soft sigh of contentment. They stayed that way for a long time, and Danni prayed silently that, no matter what happened in the future, she'd be allowed to hold this memory, this feeling, forever.

Finally, he touched his cheek softly to her temple, then

pressed his lips gently to her forehead once, twice, before whispering, "Ah, Danni ... Danni, I do love you."

She knew her hopeful heart was mirrored in her eyes when she answered him. "But hasn't it happened awfully fast Logan?"

His smile deepened even more and the adoring look on his face made Danni feel faint with the sweetness of the moment. "Not really, sweetheart," he said softly. "At least, it doesn't seem like it to me. I knew I was a goner your first night back in town, when you curled up under that old blanket on the couch in my office and glared at me for a solid hour." His words turned lightly teasing. "Yeah, I knew right then I was in serious trouble." His arms tightened around her as he murmured into the tousled waves of her hair, "Danni—I didn't mean to come on so rough a minute ago—"

She started to object, but he silenced her with a gentle finger over her lips. "No, listen. We haven't talked about this yet, but we need to. I want you to know ... about Teresa." His eyes clouded with memory as he began to explain, his hands clasping her shoulders as he spoke.

"She was the first person I ever really loved—and the first person who ever truly loved me, and accepted me for just what I was. We were happy together, and I would have gone on loving her forever, if ...." His words fell away, and instead of the jealousy Danni might have expected to feel, she knew only an overwhelming sense of sadness for him, for all he had lost.

"She died in my arms—in the middle of a shopping mall, surrounded by strangers. She bled to death. And the whole time she was dying, she just lay there, pleading with her eyes for me to help her." Anguish wrung his words from him in tight, uneven breaths. "I couldn't do a thing but hold her ... while she died." His arms around her tightened, and she felt him slump tiredly against her.

Danni lifted her face to him, openly revealing all the love she felt for him in her eyes. Her fingers were unsteady as she framed his strong, softly bearded face between her hands. "Oh, Logan, don't—you don't have to tell me any more—"

But he clasped her shoulders even more tightly, his eyes on fire with emotion. "Danni—she wanted to live. She wanted to go on being a teacher and have babies and do all the things we'd planned to do. But it was all taken away from her; she never had a chance." He lowered his face toward her, his voice softening. "But you do. That's what made me so angry, when I thought about you deliberately risking your life . . . to get a story. You don't have to do that, and I'm asking you *not* to do it!"

"Logan, please, try to understand—"

His eyes blazed, not with anger but with what appeared to be a burning determination to make her agree with him. "Promise me," he demanded, "that you won't go back to the Colony. Not for any reason."

Dismayed, she stared up at him, "But, Logan, I *have* to go back—"

"*No!*" His features contorted into an agonized plea. "Listen to me, Danni—just . . . listen, please. Someone is on to you—or at least suspicious of you—I'd bet on it. Your house has been ransacked twice, remember? All this stuff that you've shown me—what if someone else knows about it?"

Danni hadn't even thought of what he was suggesting. The fear that crossed his face was mirrored in her eyes as Logan continued, "Don't you see? You could be in real danger."

"But there's no reason to think they'd actually *harm* me, Logan, even if—"

"*They've already killed three people!*" The force of his unexpected exclamation cut through Danni's wavering feelings.

"What do you mean?"

He nearly pulled her to the table by the couch. "These lab reports . . . . " He snatched the printouts and stuck them under her nose. "They're a record of drug experiments on various individuals—including two men who have died on the premises. There's probably a record on the third one somewhere. You'll have to give me a few hours so I can study them in depth, but I'm almost sure of what I'm going to find, based on the drugs they've apparently been using. Right now it's no more than an educated guess, but something tells me that Kendrick, Jennings and Tiergard died either from being overdosed or because somebody's experiments backfired."

Danni stiffened as the full impact of his words sunk in. "Experiments . . . " she mouthed softly. "You can tell that—from those files?"

He nodded, tossing the printouts back onto the table. "What it looks like," he said, pointing to the papers, "is that the mad Dr. Sutherland has been dosing some of the elderly guests, probably just enough at first to make them coopera-tive. Apparently their monthly checks have been signed over to the Colony and deposited in different bank accounts all over the state. But according to some of the entries in those files—and Sutherland identifies himself as the writer—he experimented with some real mind-benders. I'd need the final log entries to prove it, but it surely looks as though his experiments killed those men."

"But you need proof?" she asked thoughtfully.

"And I'll get it," he stated in a low, tight tone. "Somewhere in that infirmary, there's most likely another disk like these with the final results. Sutherland seems just crazy enough to keep a record of his failures, as well as his successes."

Danni felt reasonably certain he was right. But just as quickly, she realized that Logan couldn't possibly get safely in and out of the infirmary. His very presence on the grounds, even in the parking lot, would put Ra and his assistants on alert. No, there was no way Logan could get what he needed without putting his life on the line.

But I can, Danni realized with strange calm. *The same way I got copies of the other disks. No one's going to even raise an eyebrow at my being on the grounds after hours ... it's already an established fact that I'm a workaholic. They're used to seeing my car there late at night. All I need is one more trip to the infirmary ... just one. I'll get what I need for a dynamite story, and get Logan's proof, too. If he's right about what's going on out there, we can close their doors and wrap up the election for him at the same time ... not to mention getting rid of this charge of "police brutality...."*

"Whatever you're thinking, forget it," Logan interrupted her thoughts harshly. "I don't like the look on your face."

She smiled up at him. "Are you going to tell me you read minds, too?"

"Don't I wish?" he murmured, studying her face. "Danni," he said firmly, "I want your word you won't try to go back to the Colony."

She caught her lower lip between her front teeth and looked away from him. A low growl of frustration escaped him as he pulled her more closely against him. "*Promise* me you won't do anything stupid," he ordered, frowning sternly down into her eyes.

She hesitated only a second. "I won't do anything stupid," she said evenly. *Oh, Logan, what I have to do isn't stupid ... it's absolutely essential ... for both of us ... and for so many other people, too ... I really don't have any choice....*

153

17

Fifteen minutes after Logan left, Danni was still pacing the living room floor, trying to decide exactly what to do—and when to do it. But deep inside her, she knew she had already made her decision. Her cover could be blown at any moment, and she would end up empty-handed, with no story and no proof to help Logan. There was simply too much at stake, too much that could go wrong. She must go back. Tonight.

She stopped walking, drew a deep, shaky breath, and began to formulate a plan. She would have to go to her office first, turn on lights, toss some papers around—make it look as though she were working before she tried to get into the infirmary again. What if someone saw her on the grounds at this time of night? She shook her head. A brief explanation that she'd left early this afternoon and had forgotten some files she needed would easily take care of that. There was always work to take home.

Ah, but what if one of the orderlies had found the unlocked window in the infirmary by now and secured it? That was her only way in . . . . *Don't try to tie it up too neatly, kid . . . just go with the flow and hope for the best. And while you're at it, why don't we slow this thing down long enough to ask for the Lord's help?*

She dropped to her knees by the couch and spent a few quiet moments in prayer, including a plea for Logan and his understanding. *I know he asked me not to go back, Father . . . and I don't want to go back. I'm scared to death of being discovered—but I have to go, just one more time. Please—please help me get out of there with the proof Logan needs to put Ra and the rest of them out of business. Help me get the facts I need to finish this story, to get the truth into print before anyone else is hurt by them ... Oh, dear Lord, you know I can't do this; I'll lose my nerve for sure unless you're in this with me all the way ... You've led me into this, let me be the kind of Christian who gets involved ... help me do this—for you ... and for Logan ....*

It was almost too easy, Danni thought, at least so far. She'd turned on all the lights in her office, booted up her word processor and filled half a screen with notes on a projected advertising proposal. Her desk was messy enough to look busy, so she left it just as it was. She had already killed half an hour; if anyone had been curious about her presence, they would have shown up by now.

There was no need to stall any longer. Nothing would be different if she were to wait another hour. Her chest felt tight, her hands clammy as she slipped into her denim jacket.

Since it was after hours, there was no sign of anyone on the grounds, but she was still thankful for the thick veil of clouds that draped the night in a protective shroud of darkness. Her mind was racing all the way to the infirmary. What if the window was locked? What if she had to come back tomorrow? How would she recognize the incriminating disks even if she found them? What if .... *Stop it, St. John! One step at a time ... first you get in. That's all you think about for now, getting in.*

It was a replay of the last time, right down to the pail she used to hoist herself up to the window. And the window was still unlocked. She leaped like a cat onto the inside floor. Quickly scanning the examining room, she then checked out the waiting room. When she returned, she flashed the penlight's narrow glow onto the disk containers, holding her breath as she tried first one then the others. She felt her stomach lurch and her temples begin to throb with sharp zigzags of pain. The containers were locked. All of them.

She stood staring at them blankly for a long moment, trying to think. Picking locks hadn't been included in her journalism school curriculum. Still, they didn't look to be terribly secure, no more than those dinky little diary locks that never seemed to keep anyone out. She straightened her glasses on the bridge of her nose and walked about the room, flashing the beam of the penlight here and there in search of a potential lockpick.

Bending over a white utility table, she rotated the light across a few scattered utensils, her gaze drawn to a pair of surgical scissors. She picked it up with a hopeful skip of her heart.

Securing the penlight between her teeth to free her hands, she tried the third container in the row because it housed the other disks she'd copied. Almost disbelievingly, she felt the lock give when she jimmied it with the scissors. With the penlight still in her mouth, she searched hurriedly through the container with both hands, choking off a groan of frustration when she found no disks with labels that even remotely resembled those of the other disks she'd copied.

A snap outside the window made her very nearly drop the penlight from her mouth, but she caught it just in time and doused the light. She tiptoed cautiously to a spot where she could peer out the window without being seen, but saw nothing. Still, she waited, standing rigidly for several minutes before expelling a relieved breath and returning to the disk containers.

The second lock gave almost as easily as the first one, but she could have cried with exasperation when the disks turned out to be clearly labeled inventory files and bookkeeping records. That left only one more container, fastened with the most stubborn lock of the three. She pried at it with the scissors a full five minutes before it finally gave way. By this time, her hands were shaking almost uncontrollably.

But her perseverance was rewarded. In the back of the container, shoved behind all the other disks, was one disk with a small plain label bearing only the word *Inactive*. Danni had no way of knowing whether this was what she was looking for, but she grabbed it and, retrieving her shoulder bag from the floor where she'd tossed it earlier, carefully tucked the disk into a side flap and slung the bag over her shoulder.

Replacing the scissors on the utility table, she darted one quick glance around the room before climbing out the window and making her way back to the *Standard* offices.

Once inside her office, she collapsed weakly onto her desk chair, not even bothering to remove her jacket. Her breathing was labored and uneven, and she automatically reached inside her purse for her asthma medication, placing it on the desk where she could reach it quickly if necessary. Then, for a couple of moments, she allowed herself to simply sink into the chair and try to relax.

Relief washed over her as she realized what a foolhardy escapade the past hour had actually been, and that she would have had absolutely no recourse if anyone had walked in on her. *Lord, I probably don't even deserve your protection when I do something that dumb ... but thank you all the same.*

And so now she would leave the Colony for the last time. She could already feel the enormous load of tension she'd been carrying all day begin to drain from her, just knowing she wouldn't have to come back. Even if she didn't have the disk she needed, there was no way she could return, not now. Undoubtedly her office lights had been seen by someone tonight, so her presence on the grounds would be known. And when the forced locks on the disk containers were discovered, she was reasonably sure suspicion would be cast in her direction. No. Story or no story, she had to leave and begin to put together the pieces of the puzzle, praying she had enough to complete the picture.

Slowly, she roused herself and collected a few personal items from her desk, shoving them haphazardly into her briefcase, then turned off her word processor. Sighing wearily, she stood and with a movement born of habit pushed a few loose papers into a stack, then closed the bottom drawer of the desk.

She took one long look around the room, taking grim pleasure in the fact that it would be her *last* look. She was reaching for the wall switch to turn off the office lights when a voice at her back stopped her dead. "More overtime, Sister?"

She stiffened, her mind clamoring in an effort to thwart the wave of fear sweeping over her. She whirled around to see Reverend Ra standing just behind her in the doorway. Suddenly he was inside, followed by Brother Penn and the larger of the two orderlies who worked at the infirmary. As the three of them approached her, she retreated into the middle of the office.

She came close to screaming but knew her only hope was to appear unperturbed and totally innocent. This wasn't a social call on Ra's part, not when he was accompanied by the others.

"I'm afraid so," she said, trying for an even tone of voice. "I took a few hours off this afternoon, and now I'm paying for it." Danni's smile felt like plastic, but she forced herself to keep it in place.

"How very commendable," Ra said smoothly, matching her brittle smile with a wooden one of his own. He walked toward her, his floor-length white robe whispering as he moved.

"You know, Sister," he purred, extending one hand outward, palm up, "you are undoubtedly the most dedicated, hardworking employee I've ever had."

He was close enough now for Danni to see that his eyes blazed with some unholy, threatening fire. "That makes your— termination—even more regrettable."

She forced herself to stare up at him, refusing to allow the menace in his tone to cower her. "My termination?"

Flanked by Penn, whose face was a tight mask of anger, and the same orderly who had given Danni the aspirin in the infirmary, Ra stood quietly, looking down into her face, studying her with what appeared to be clinical curiosity. "Let me correct that, Sister. It is, in fact, *D. Stuart James* we shall be terminating, is it not?"

Danni moistened her lips nervously, realizing with an oppressive slam of panic against her chest that Logan's fears had apparently come to pass. "I'm afraid I don't understand—"

"Oh, of *course* you do," Ra quickly contradicted her in a voice thick with sarcasm. "Why, a sharp little newshound like yourself doesn't miss a beat, I'm sure."

Knowing it was futile, sickly aware that she was trapped, Danni nevertheless made one more try. "Look, I'm really tired," she said firmly, starting to move away from Ra and his henchmen, "so if it's all right with you, I'll just call it a day and—"

He caught her by the neck so abruptly and so roughly she cried out. "Save it," he ordered, the calm, syrupy voice of Reverend Ra suddenly replaced by an alien harshness. "You're calling it a day all right, but not the way you'd like." He nodded shortly to the orderly. "Take her to the infirmary."

"No!" Danni screamed in desperation, lashing out with her arms to block the big, rough-looking orderly. But his burly arms were already locked around her middle as he half-drug her from the room. Ra and Penn followed behind them.

She struggled wildly, screaming with all the strength she could muster. Just for a moment, the noise stopped them.

"Shut her up!" grated Ra angrily. The orderly clamped one big hand over her mouth, still holding her securely with his other hand. Danni bit at the hand over her mouth, trying desperately to remember at least one of the moves Logan had taught during her two karate classes. But she was almost irrational with terror and unable to think.

Her lungs screamed for air, and she choked and coughed, trying for a deep breath. *Not now, oh, please, Lord, don't let me have an attack now!* Sobbing and gulping, she heaved once, then again, feeling a stab of sick relief when the precious air filled her lungs and expelled again. After one more breath, she felt a glimmer of memory sweep across her mind. Desperately forcing herself into a position where she could negotiate a solid elbow attack or at least a low kick, she managed to free herself from the thick forearm around her middle. At the same time, she rammed into him with a sharp elbow attack that knocked him breathless for just an instant. But he was a big, rock-hard man, and Danni was too small and inexperienced in the art of self-defense to keep her momentum going. Within two or three seconds, the orderly recovered, and grasped her in an even tighter hold than before, pushing her brutally out the door of the *Standard* building and strong-arming her all the way to the infirmary.

18

Danni came as close to hysteria as she'd ever been in her life when they shoved her roughly through the infirmary door and pushed her into the brightly lighted examining room. It was at that moment she encountered the watery, expressionless gaze of Dr. Sutherland.

She screamed silently. This man frightened her even more than Ra. Being trapped in the same room with the two of them had the effect of temporarily unhinging all rational thought. Frozen in place, Danni could only stare at the doctor. He stood unmoving, wearing a smudged white lab coat, both hands clasped together in front of him, an oddly placid gesture for the circumstances.

His mouth thinned in a chilling rictus of a smile. "Help her onto an examining table, please, Curtis."

Danni's heart went crazy, pounding so wildly against her ribs she thought her chest would explode. But somehow, in the midst of her terror, she forced her voice to work, at the same time making a futile attempt to twist out of the orderly's hands. "Leave me alone!"

Reverend Ra smoothly interposed himself between Danni and the doctor. "Now, now, Miss St. John—it is *St. John*, isn't it—not *James*? What you need to do here, I believe, is cooperate." His voice was undulgently soothing, and Danni had never in her life wanted so much to strike out at a man as she did at this moment.

"No one is going to harm you in any way," he continued, infuriating Danni even more with his benevolent smile. "You are, after all, a member of our *family* now."

Something cold and deadening seeped through Danni.

"What are you talking about?"

He tilted his head to one side, lifting his silver brows and widening his eyes in mock surprise. "Why, Sister, you haven't forgotten, have you?"

At Danni's silent glare, he reached out and touched her on the shoulder, making her cringe. "You *have* forgotten! My, you young people today simply *astonish* me with your thoughtlessness! It's been only hours since you expressed your desire to disassociate yourself with your old life and join the rest of the family here at the Colony." He clutched her shoulder more tightly.

Danni looked into the oily, malevolent eyes smiling down at her and knew the most penetrating chill of horror she'd ever experienced. "What are you talking about?" she challenged hoarsely.

His expression remained blandly agreeable as he moved his hand from her shoulder to lightly pat her cheek. "Now, don't you worry, Sister. The only thing you're to concern yourself with for the next few hours is getting some much needed rest. We'll make all the necessary arrangements for you to join us."

An ugly, dark suspicion rolled itself into a terrifying ball of certainty, assaulting Danni's mind. "What—what do you mean?" Her voice was shaking as badly as the rest of her body, but at least she could still speak.

"We're deeply concerned about you, Sister," Ra answered with a hypocritical frown of concern. "We know all about the long hours you've been working lately, the way you've pushed yourself. I've told you before, dedication is admirable, but you simply must take better care of yourself. Now then," he said firmly, "you just let Curtis help you onto the table, like a good girl. The doctor is simply going to give you a little something to calm your nerves and help you rest."

Danni jerked, trying desperately to twist herself free, but it

162

only made the orderly tighten his grip. "You're crazy!" she shouted. "You can't do this—you can't possibly think you're going to get away with something like this—"

Her frightened outburst was quickly cut off by the orderly's hand over her mouth. "Put her on the table," Ra ordered sharply with a small nod. "And make sure she stays there," he added significantly.

With disbelieving horror, Danni felt herself lifted from the floor as though she were a child and carried across the room. The orderly deposited her on one of the white-sheeted examining tables and immediately secured her hands and feet to each side of the frame with the heavy cloth restraints.

Through a haze of terror, Danni absorbed only the bare essentials of what was happening to her. She had the odd sensation that she was watching a fast-moving video of the entire scene, while searching desperately for a way to turn it off.

In spite of her emotional turmoil and the murky confusion of her mind, she wasn't surprised when she felt herself begin to wheeze. At first it was no more than a warning shortness of breath. She fought for control, but was so close to completely losing her grip on reality she could manage only a weak, silent plea for help ... *Father, don't let them do this ... break into this nightmare for me ... Oh, Father, help me ... please help me ....*

She was dimly aware of Penn leaving the room, ordered by Ra to search her office. Danni glanced at the doctor who was doing something at the sink. He turned and moved to her side when the sound of her labored breathing grew more noticeable. Ra, too, approached her, his eyes narrowing with speculation. "What's wrong with her?"

Sutherland looked down at her with all the interest of a butcher assessing a side of beef. "Apparently she's asthmatic." He waited a moment, then added, "Fear or stress often brings on an attack."

Danni turned her head quickly when she heard the door open, and through a blur of bewilderment she felt a sudden explosion of hope. She saw the uniform first, and squeezed her eyes shut against the hot tears of relief welling up. *Logan! Everything was going to be all right now!* But when she opened her eyes, she saw a crazy, contorted screen that threatened her sanity.

For the uniform belonged, not to Logan, but to Philip Rider. *But that's all right... at least he's here, at least he's the law... probably Logan is right outside—*

And then she saw him flash a pointed look at Ra, a look that quickly changed to a lazy, sardonic smile as he came to stand by her. She felt a jolt of sick disbelief. The awful significance of how wrong she'd been dawned on her when she saw that he was holding in one upraised hand her purse-sized tube of medication, the one she had left on her desk earlier. In his other hand was the disk she'd taken from the infirmary and tucked inside her shoulder bag.

"I think this is what the lady needs," Rider drawled, as Danni wheezed for breath, hope and desperation in her eyes. But when she saw him standing over her, passing the medication back and forth in front of her face in a playful, mocking gesture as his smile turned to a sneer, she knew an overwhelming sense of blood-freezing fear.

She shook her head as though it would clear the confusion of the scene, but nothing changed. The three of them—the deputy, the doctor, and Ra—stood around the table that held her captive, discussing her with total indifference to her presence. The enormous circle of light overhead seemed to be shrinking, and the ring of voices around her sounded muddy and distant. She was fighting for breath, feeling the lack of oxygen now, knowing she'd either choke to death or pass out at any moment. She had a distorted, fleeting thought, an image quickly gone of

Logan's face, the soft, caring smile he'd worn when she'd last seen him. *Oh, Logan . . . why didn't I do what you asked? Why didn't I listen to you?*

Somehow, from the quicksand she was drowning in, she saw the deputy's smirk turn to menace. "For such a little thing, you've caused some pretty big trouble here, Miss St. John." He handed the tube of medication to the doctor on the other side of the table. "Give her what she needs. Then put her out for the rest of the night. I need some time to tear her house apart and find out just how much she knows. I was in too much of a hurry the other times."

He started to walk away, then turned back to the doctor. "Don't let anything happen to her yet. Not until she answers some questions for me tomorrow. Just keep her quiet."

With a mocking twist of his mouth, he raked his gaze over Danni once more. "Honey, you got mixed up with the wrong cop," he said softly. "I could have done you a sight more good than Cousin Logan."

As he turned and swaggered out of the room, the doctor placed the tube of medication close to Danni's open mouth and released just enough to enable her to begin breathing. But when she saw the doctor remove a hypodermic syringe from a small table nearby, her barely audible cry quickly faded. Within seconds after she felt the needle pierce the tender skin of her forearm, she surrendered to the whispering, warm darkness that had been waiting to claim her.

19

Somebody was playing a record at the wrong speed across the room. Strangely enough, the dragging, slurred voices blended perfectly with the slow rotation of the circular white light above Danni's head. She wondered dully why her head felt so heavy. Her temples ached with the effort of every movement, no matter how slight. There was an uneasy, tremulous feeling in the pit of her stomach, too. She hoped she wasn't coming down with the flu.

Her eyes were so heavy . . . she was too weak to keep them open any longer . . . she must be very ill . . . she would just sleep awhile . . . perhaps she'd feel better later . . . .

No . . . she needed to stay awake . . . the voices on the slow-speed record were talking about her. *Why are these people in my bedroom? Must stay awake; they're discussing me for some reason . . . Doctor . . . there's a doctor here? Am I that ill, that Logan brought me a doctor? Logan . . . he's not here . . . where is he . . . Logan . . . .*

"Logan?" The sound of her voice, faint as it was, brought Ra and Dr. Sutherland to the side of the examining table. "What'd she say?" the orderly hunched in a nearby chair asked.

The fog gradually lifted from Danni's mind, and in its place came a throbbing onslaught of pain in her head.

"She's calling for her boyfriend. The sheriff." Why did Reverend Ra sound so disgusted with her?

"When is Rider coming back? She's going to be completely lucid soon. Should I put her under again?"

Dr. Sutherland? What's he doing here? Why would Logan call him? He knows that man gives me the creeps . . . .

"No. You'd better leave her as she is. Rider wants to question her. She's not going anywhere." The record's speed gradually accelerated to normal. *Reverend Ra!* Danni opened her eyes again. The light wasn't rotating any longer. *I'm not at home! I'm ... oh, no! No ... no, please ... I'm still in the infirmary ....*

The events of the past night came rushing back, hurling themselves against her consciousness like furiously raging tidal waves, the impact of what had happened launching a full-scale assault against her reason. *I can't give in to this ... somehow I've got to keep my senses ... I have to stay calm ... I can't panic ....* She closed her eyes, hoping to shut out the reality—or at least some of the madness—of the situation she was in.

"Look, Milo, I don't think—"

"I told you *never* to call me that! I ... am ... *Reverend Ra* ... to you and to everyone else here, can't you get that through that junked-up head of yours?!"

"Sorry," the doctor muttered resentfully. "What do you intend to do with her?"

"I've already explained that!" Ra's voice was harsh with impatience. "You're getting to be as much of a zombie as the rest of these vegetables, Victor! If you have an ounce of brains left, you'll lay off that stuff! You're no good to me if you can't think!" His next words were slow and deliberately ominous. "And this is the end of the road for you. If you can't cut it here, you're finished."

Danni heard a muffled sound of assent from the doctor before Ra continued, in a somewhat more civil tone. "Once Rider's through with her, you can inject her with the same concoction you use for the senior citizens. She'll simply meld into the rest of the group. I intend to keep her working on the paper as long as she's able to function. Certainly until we milk for all it's worth the fact that a crusading Christian journalist has left *her* church for *ours!*" He hesitated an instant, then laughed unpleasantly. "We should be able to get an absolutely *brilliant* editorial from her in support of Carey Hilliard for sheriff!"

Nausea boiled up in Danni's throat. *No, Lord, please . . . I'd rather they kill me!* Only sheer strength of will kept her from giving in to hysteria. She forced herself to keep her eyes shut, not wanting them to know she was fully conscious.

" . . . and you be very sure there are no . . . *accidents* with this one, Victor!"

The doctor actually whined when he answered. "I told you it wasn't my fault. I didn't know they were taking other medication—"

"Oh, save it! Just be sure you know what you're doing this time!"

A heavy, sickening dread threatened to cut off Danni's breath, but she ground her teeth together and silently pleaded for help. *Send Logan . . . oh, please, Lord, send Logan to get me out of this . . . don't give them the victory . . . don't let them use me to further their evil against you . . . .*

She cracked her eyes open when the door slammed. *Add!* The boy walked in, glanced from the doctor and the orderly to Ra, started to speak, then saw Danni on the examining table. His mouth agape, he started toward her. "Miss St. John! What's wrong? What happened to you?"

She saw the doctor reach out and grab his arm, halting his movement. "She's very ill. You're not to be in here!"

Ra stepped in at that instant, turning on his paternal charm. "She'll be fine, Brother Add. But she *does* need medical attention. Unfortunately, our young sister here hasn't yet learned to pace herself. Her dedication to the *Standard* has worn her out." He rested a large hand on the teenager's shoulder, lowering his voice to a conspiratorial murmur. "I'm afraid she's dangerously close to a physical— and perhaps emotional—breakdown. Dr. Sutherland will be giving her his personal attention. You realize, of course, that while she's ill, we'll be depending on you to keep the paper going for us. We *can* count on you, can't we, Brother?"

With a confused, troubled expression, the boy darted a look from his leader to Danni. "Yes, Reverend Ra, I'll do whatever I can."

Danni took a deep breath and fought to lift her head from the table. "Add! Help me!"

A look of alarm washed across Add's features. His gaze took in the frowning orderly, the glare of Dr. Sutherland, and the commiserating sigh of Reverend Ra who turned to Danni.

"They're holding me against my will, Add! They drugged me! Oh, Add—please! Call Sheriff McGarey!"

With his back to the others, the doctor bent down to Danni. Hovering only inches away from her face, he whispered menacingly, "If you don't shut up, I'll give you an injection you'll never come out of!"

Add cast a concerned glance her way, then began speaking in hushed tones with Ra.

"Reverend Ra, the reason I came to find Dr. Sutherland was to ask what I should do about a vagrant I picked up in the van this morning."

"A vagrant, son?"

"Yes, sir. An elderly man. He was hitchhiking out on Highway 72 earlier when I went into town to get the kerosene refilled. He nearly fell in front of the van. He's either sick or drunk. I can't tell which."

Ra clucked sympathetically. "We'll have to tend to him, of course. Where is he now?"

"In the parking lot, sir, still in the van. He's conscious, but I think he's delirious or something."

"Mm. All right, let's get you some help." Turning to the orderly, Ra beckoned him away from his post by Danni. "Brother Add needs some assistance with an older gentleman out in the parking lot, Curtis. Would you go with him, please, and bring him here so the doctor can examine him?"

Danni murmured Add's name once, weakly, before he went out the door, followed by the orderly. But if the boy heard her, he didn't acknowledge it.

The door opened again within seconds, but Danni lay still, lifelessly staring at the ceiling. It was only when she heard Ra grumble, "About time," that she turned to see who had entered the room. When she did, the chill in her spine grew even colder.

Rider didn't stop until he reached her side. His dark gray eyes impaled her as a humorless smile crossed his face. "You have been *very* busy, little lady," he sneered. Bending over her he pulled her cassette recorder out of the pocket of his leather jacket.

Danni's gaze followed the movement silently, then returned to his face.

He studied her with a look of amused contempt. "I'll give you this—you've got more than your share of nerve." Tucked under his other arm was the portfolio containing the photocopied articles and press cards identifying Danni St. John as D. Stuart James. He tossed them at Ra.

"The motive behind the lady's madness would seem to be the stuff of which headlines are made," he said glibly. "She was going to smear you all over the papers, Reverend. Spill all your secrets and put you right out of business."

Ra approached the examining table. "What did you find out?"

"Enough," Rider snapped. "She's an expose reporter. Crusader type. Why, she's even let herself get beat up for a story. Brave little thing. You wouldn't have had a chance against a tiger like her, Reverend. You'd be back to selling non-existent lots in Florida."

"Now, listen here, Rider—"

The deputy's smooth voice cracked like a gunshot. "No,

you listen. This sweet little Dixie dahlia has enough information to lock you away." He flashed a furious glare at the doctor. "Thanks to Dr. Frankenstein's sloppy lab records, she knows about Kendrick and the others. *And*," he paused for effect, "she's got copies of the monthly bank deposits."

"How—what are you talking about?"

Rider pulled a crumpled wad of paper from the portfolio. "Apparently she got hold of some of your disks. Here's her own personal printout." He handed the paper to Ra with a pointed look.

The rage on the big, white-robed man's face after he scanned the printout was enough to make Danni recoil. "You little—"

The deputy's hand snaked out and caught Ra by the arm. "Save your righteous anger. It's a little late. Just listen. This babe is trouble—real trouble. You're going to have to deal with her. And what worries me even more, I don't know how much she may have told my hardnosed cousin."

"McGarey?" For the first time since she'd met the man, Danni saw a look bordering on fear cross Ra's face.

Rider nodded. "Seems as though they've got a thing going. I have this uncomfortable feeling that he might know just about everything *she* knows." He turned back to Danni. "What about it, short stuff? Have you dumped all this on Logan?"

Danni hesitated, then shook her head back and forth. "He doesn't know anything," she protested.

Rider appraised her for several seconds, then smiled maliciously. "You're lying, lady. I'd bet on it." He whirled around to Ra, who was still hovering nearby, looking anxiously from Danni to the deputy. "Logan was to go to Scottsboro early this morning. I'm going into town and see if I can find anything in his desk that'll tell us what he knows."

He pointed to Danni over his shoulder. "Keep her right

where she is, and give her enough stuff so she can't talk to anybody. I've got to find out how much Logan knows. We may have bigger problems than I thought."

He turned on his heel and walked quickly out of the room, leaving Ra to stand over Danni, fixing her with a resentful, threatening stare. Without looking away from her, he barked to the doctor, "Put her out again. Give her enough so I don't have to worry about her opening her mouth for several hours."

Danni looked anxiously at the doctor, who went obediently to the supply cabinet and began to prepare an injection. Tears of frustration and helplessness spilled over onto her cheeks. When the door opened, she saw Ra shake his head at Sutherland in a gesture of warning to put the hypodermic away.

Add entered first, holding the door for the orderly, who was half-carrying a disreputable looking elderly man who appeared to be unconscious.

"He's in bad shape, Doc," the orderly said, easily lifting the man off his feet and onto one of the examining tables close to Danni. "I think he's sick. I don't smell any liquor on him."

"All right, Curtis, be careful with him. Get a blanket for him, too," Ra ordered. He walked over to inspect the slender, unmoving form on the table, wrinkling his nose in disgust at the man's filthy overalls and hunting jacket. "You'll have to clean him up," he told the orderly. "He smells like something dead."

"Yes, sir," the big, slow-moving orderly replied, retrieving a blanket from the linen closet and covering the man. "I noticed that."

Danni studied the man lying on the table next to her as much as she could from her position. He *was* dirty. In fact, he was absolutely grimy. He looked as though he hadn't washed for days, and the gray hair falling over his eyes from beneath a squashed hunting cap was pathetically oily and stringy. Danni felt no revulsion, only pity for the poor unfortunate who was totally oblivious to the threatening predicament he was in.

Her gaze moved to Add, surprised to see him still standing near the doorway watching her with an expression that seemed to reflect a deep well of feeling. Danni couldn't blame him for turning his back on her earlier. She'd been foolish to hope even for a moment that he might have more loyalty toward her than the *Master Guide*. Ra inspired an awesome mixture of devotion and trust in his followers. Add was just another victim. She made a feeble attempt to smile at the boy, but Add had shifted his attention to Reverend Ra.

"You can go along now, son. We'll take care of this gentleman, whoever he is," Ra was saying kindly. "Oh—did you see if he has any identification on him? We need to know if there's anyone we should call . . . . "

He jerked around when the door burst open and Rider charged in, his uniform hat tilted back on his head. "I saw you bring someone in when I was pulling out of the parking lot. What's going on?" Without waiting for an answer, he pushed himself into the space between the two examining tables, looking at the man who lay motionless beside Danni.

"It's just another derelict," Ra said carelessly. "He's out cold. Don't worry about it."

Danni glanced from the deputy's face to the old man on the table, then back at Rider, wondering at the crimson flush creeping over his features.

"You *idiot*!" He turned on Ra and the orderly, whose dull gaze cleared somewhat.

"Wh—what's wrong?" Ra took a step toward the table, the orderly right behind him.

Suddenly the elderly man dived off the table. Add flung

the door open, and Logan charged through the entrance like a dark, unleashed tornado looking for a place to land. The deputy's words were almost lost in the din . . . .

"That's no derelict! That's Tucker Wells, Logan's sidekick—"

20

Logan, his gun aimed directly at his cousin, didn't stop moving until he was well into the midst of the stunned group. In his dive from the table, Tucker hit the orderly full-force just below his knees. A calculated karate punch knocked the wind out of him and sent him sprawling, face down, long enough for Tucker to handcuff him to the metal support of the computer table.

Too dazed to utter a sound after her initial cry of surprise, Danni watched in amazement as Logan, his gun never wavering from its focus on Philip Rider, threw a precision elbow attack with his free arm at Ra, causing him to reel crazily. Tucker, finished with the orderly, grabbed a thick piece of gauze from its roll on a nearby utility table and tied Ra to a chair before heading for the doctor.

Sutherland, however, had already begun to move toward Danni with the hypodermic syringe he'd filled earlier held high in one hand. Before either Logan or Tucker could get to her, Danni felt his hand around her throat, nearly choking her in his rough grasp. "I'll kill her!" he screamed wildly, waving the syringe over her head like a madman. "Just stop where you are, or she's dead, I'm warning you!"

Logan, pivoting so he could keep his gun trained on Philip, appraised the hysterical doctor. Tucker stopped dead a few feet away from the disabled Ra, squinting narrowly from Logan to Sutherland.

"All right . . . all right, now . . . " babbled the doctor, his face bathed in perspiration, his eyes glassy with fright. "Add," everyone looked at the boy standing quietly by the door, "you take the sheriff's gun and bring it to me."

The boy blinked his dark eyes rapidly a few times, pressed his lips tightly together, and started toward Logan.

"Don't do it, son," Tucker said quietly as Add passed him.

But Add didn't stop until he faced Logan, the two of them making eye contact for a long moment before the boy extended one trembling hand palm upward for the gun. Danni's hopes plummeted when she saw Logan hand the gun over without a word.

"That's fine, boy," the doctor crooned in a singsong voice as Add walked toward him with the gun. "Bring it here, now, that's fine."

Add didn't so much as glance at Danni as he approached, but instead walked around the side of the examining table to where Sutherland was standing behind her head.

Suddenly, in a movement so lightning fast Danni would never remember seeing it, Add threw himself against the doctor, thrusting the gun into Sutherland's abdomen, and throwing out one long, thin arm to knock the hypodermic from his hand.

Logan saw what was happening and moved, whirling himself into a spinning storm of assault against Phil. He high-kicked the service revolver, which the younger man had just pulled from his holster, out of his hand. With a couple of deadly accurate punches, he sent his cousin reeling over a chair.

Tucker, grabbing Rider's gun, moved faster than Danni would have dreamed possible for a man so severely lamed. Hurling his slight body between the examining tables, he helped Add pin Sutherland against the wall.

"You did just fine, son," he panted. "Now, help the girl out of those restraints," he commanded without taking his eyes off the doctor.

Add was crying unashamedly as he struggled to free Danni from the heavy cloth ties on her hands and feet. His

176

tears fell onto the sheet covering her. "Are you all right, Miss St. John? I'm sorry—I'm so sorry I couldn't help you when I was here earlier! The sheriff made me promise not to do anything; he said I should just find out where you were and make sure the door was unlocked!" His words tumbled out between sobs, and once Danni was free, she sat up and hugged him.

"Oh, Add, Add! You called Logan!"

"No, ma'am! He called your office early this morning looking for you. When I told him you hadn't come in yet, he said you weren't at home either and he was afraid something might have happened to you, and would I check the infirmary . . . ."

"But when you were here earlier you didn't—"

The boy's words continued to bounce from his lips as though he hadn't heard her. "When I told him what they'd done to you, he told me exactly what to do, about how Mr. Wells, his friend, was going to pretend to be a vagrant, and that I should bring him here and then just stay by the door until he—Sheriff McGarey—got here—"

"Danni—are you all right?" Logan's gruff shout from where he was helping Tucker tie the doctor down on an examining table made Danni and Add jump apart.

"Yes—yes, I'm fine!"

"Add, go out to my patrol car and get Deputy Baker on the radio. He should be at the office—tell him to get out here! Have him call the state troopers, too!" He turned back to Tucker. "All right, let's take care of Phil."

Logan, grimacing with the effort, slung his dazed, moaning cousin over his shoulder and carried him to the same table where Danni had been tied only moments before. He and Tucker quickly secured the younger man, binding his hands and his feet.

Only then did Logan turn to Danni, and the parade of emotions she saw marching across his face made her catch

177

her breath. She walked over to him and Tucker, ready to throw her arms around each one of them, but stopped in front of Logan when she saw the storm boiling in his eyes.

"Get your story, Half-pint?" he growled.

"Logan—" She looked from him to Tucker, who shrugged, then winked and walked away. It was anyone's guess what was going on inside Logan's head, Danni thought, but he looked like a giant hurricane about to roll.

"Wouldn't you say you got a little carried away with the—*courage of your convictions*?" he snarled.

"You're *angry* with me!" She would never understand this man! "You crash in here and save my life, and now you're angry! I was only moments away from being murdered—or at the least being turned into some awful kind of vegetable—and you're about to *scold* me? You just wait a minute, Logan McGarey—"

The look he turned on her almost sent her to her knees. "*You* wait a minute!" he roared. "We're not talking right now! I am angry. I hurt my back. And I have just been scared out of ten years of my life! I had visions all the way out here of finding you dead or with your brains turned into mush! We'll talk *later*!"

He left her standing there with her mouth at half-mast and walked over to the examining table where Philip Rider lay. Furious as she was with him, Danni felt a pang of sympathy for the hurt etched on Logan's face as he stood, silently staring down at the sullen young deputy for a long time before speaking.

"I thought you were going to Scottsboro," Rider said sourly.

"That's exactly what I wanted you to think," Logan answered flatly. "How deep are you in, Phil? And why? Why did you do it?"

His cousin glared at him defiantly, his pouting mouth set

in a nasty scowl. "Why not?" he shot out contemptuously. "Not all of us are as noble as you, *Cousin!*"

"What's that mean?" Logan asked him quietly.

"It means *money*, Logan! It may not bother you, man, but I got sick of everybody else's castoffs all the time I was growing up! I made up my mind a long time ago I was going to take everything I could get any way I could! This town thinks we're scum anyway, so why not enjoy a few of the benefits?"

Danni saw Logan flinch. "What exactly did you do for them?" Other than the almost unnoticeable twitch of a muscle at the side of his mouth, his face appeared to be carved in granite.

Rider sneered. "Protection, mostly. Made sure no one caught on to the welfare check scam; covered their tracks when the old guys accidentally bought it—"

"Protection. Welfare . . . let me see if I've got it right, Phil," Logan interrupted. "The kids brought in vagrants who didn't have anywhere else to go. They signed over their checks to the Colony and were kept happily drugged and out of the way from then on. Right?"

Rider nodded. "No one else knew where they were, and even if they knew, they didn't care. It was perfect."

"Yeah," Logan agreed softly, "perfect. What happened to the three that died?"

The younger man lifted his brows negligently. "The mad doctor over there apparently got his formula goofed up. Something happened with their hearts. He said they must have been taking other medication, and it caused some kind of reaction when he injected them with his own zombie juice."

Add had come back into the room and was talking quietly with Tucker. Danni went to stand a little closer to Logan so she could hear his conversation with Phil, but he gave no sign that he was aware of her presence.

"How many times did you search Danni's house?"

Rider flicked his gaze over Logan's face scornfully. "What makes you think it was me?"

Logan reached down to his cousin's shirt pocket and pulled out a pair of sunglasses, turning them over a few times, then holding them up to the light as he studied them. Finally, he retrieved something from his own pocket—the small piece of metal Danni had found in her lingerie drawer. He placed it beside the temple of the sunglasses in his hand, where a piece of tape had been wrapped, apparently to cover a missing part. His tone was thoughtful, almost as though he were talking to himself. "I knew there was something familiar about this as soon as I saw it," he said. "But it didn't ring a bell until I noticed that piece of tape on your glasses yesterday."

He lifted a hand and gingerly stroked a fast-darkening bruise on his cheek. Danni ached to touch the bruise herself, but the anger she'd seen in his eyes a few minutes before stopped her.

His voice was harsh when he went on questioning Philip. "It was you who marked up Penn and Albert Weston, wasn't it?"

The younger man looked up at his cousin with belligerence. "I didn't hurt them—just roughed them up."

"I thought Weston changed his mind a little too conveniently that night. What did you threaten him with—jail?"

Rider nodded.

"And did they agree to your knocking them around or did you just go after them?"

Phil took in a deep breath, then coughed a couple of times before answering. "They didn't have any choice. Their illustrious *Master Guide*," he said with a sneer, "made it painfully clear to them that it was in the best interests of the Colony to do a smear job on you. All I had to do was throw a

180

few light punches once we got back out here that night," he explained indifferently.

Logan turned toward the cult leader, almost bumping into Danni, who looked up at him with a silent demand that he notice her. But he looked right over her head to the glowering Ra. "Tell me, *Reverend*," he said caustically, "what's your real name?"

"Milo Cavendar," inserted Danni quickly.

Logan looked down at her, studying her face for what seemed like a very long time. Finally, one dark brow quirked, and Danni was pretty sure he was tempted to smile. He didn't, of course. *Brave Eagle* would never smile in the face of the enemy. "Milo Cavendar?" he repeated, still scanning her features.

"That's right. I did my homework before I took this assignment. He's also been known as Floyd Basil, Leonard Sprague, and Stanley Coates."

Tucker and Add came over and stood listening quietly. Again touching the bruise on his cheek, Logan's gaze drifted over Danni's tousled hair, her smudged face, and her rumpled clothing.

Something in the softening of his mouth told her she had him hooked. "He's been a securities salesman, a real estate developer, and a smut peddler. And that just covers the last ten years."

Both eyebrows lifted this time, and, yes, there was definitely the faint glimmer of a smile. In fact, his whole expression was gentling, warming to the familiar glint of amused tolerance and tender affection that made her heart race like a wild thing.

She pressed on. "He's been arrested twice for fraud, once for credit card counterfeiting, and has a whole sheet of traffic tickets on file." Feeling pretty good now, Danni decided to wrap it up. "He used to fight pit bulls, too."

When she saw Logan's mouth drop slightly open and that

wonderful, sweet softness dawn in his eyes, she decided to go for the jugular. *"And—"*

He groaned. "You're really something, aren't you?"

"—He's part Indian." Silence. "Like you."

Luckily for Danni, Deputy Baker and two state troopers came hurrying through the door at that moment.

21

"Hard to believe it'll soon be Christmas," Tucker commented later that same evening, as he refilled Danni's and Logan's cups with his unique, richly brewed coffee. "Want some more hot chocolate, son?" he asked Add, who was sitting directly across the table from Danni, dividing his attention between his new friends and the litter of Irish setter puppies scampering back and forth from the fireplace to the table.

"And I've already got my present," Danni said with a bright smile, glancing down at her feet where Chief, a fat and shiny ball of copper fur, was busily trying to bite his own tail. Sassy, his mother, rested quietly on the other side of Logan, occasionally giving her incorrigible pups a warning maternal growl.

Tucker had insisted on taking everyone out to the farm as soon as Logan and the state troopers had tied up all the loose ends at the Colony and taken their prisoners into town. "The three of you need some attention after this day," the older man told them in a voice that clearly anticipated no argument.

Nor did he get any. After fixing a wonderful meal of baked ham, browned potatoes, and cornbread, he was now pushing another brownie at Danni before sitting down to enjoy his own coffee. "What's going to happen to all those people out at the Colony now?" he asked Logan. "There must be dozens of elderly folks in addition to all the kids."

Logan took another deep sip of coffee and inclined his head toward Danni, beside him. "She thinks she's got that all figured out."

183

Tired as she was, excitement bubbled in Danni's eyes when she answered. "I'm going to contact people from the local churches and see if they'll help. The grounds and the facilities are perfect as a shelter for troubled teens. And I'll just bet a lot of those elderly people would thrive on the responsibility of helping take care of the buildings and the kids. Of course," she added quickly, "for those who don't want to stay there, we'll try to find homes and employment for them."

"I'd enjoy helping out with the young people, Danni," Tucker said quietly. "I have a fondness for teenagers." He smiled at Add, and the boy gave him a shy, pleased look.

"What do you intend to use for money?" asked Logan, ever the cynic.

"The 'Family Bank,' I hope," Danni replied without hesitation. "Of course, the courts will have to administer it. There must be a lot of money—taken in from the young people and the elderly—tied up in banks all over the state. That would give us a start. And we can invest some of it. Later, we can try to get support from the churches."

She was surprised when Logan, leaning back in his chair with his arms crossed over his chest, said, "I don't think you'll have any problem with that."

"You don't?"

He shook his head. "No. When they find out what's really been going on out there, I think you'll get whatever you need."

Danni stared up at him. "That's quite a departure from your former way of thinking, isn't it?"

Logan didn't reply for a long moment. When he did, his words came slowly. "I s'pose it is. I may have expected a little too much a few years ago. I guess it's difficult for people, when they can't see for themselves what's going on, to just jump into a situation and act. Once they know the truth, though, I think they'll help you."

Surprised by his words, Danni's expression was more serious than usual. "But , Logan, you were right—well, at least partly. A lot of terrible things could be stopped before they ever got off the ground if people weren't so reluctant to get involved."

"I still believe that," he agreed quickly, "but what I did was to lump everyone in the same bowl." He smiled at her, and the tenderness in his eyes made Danni flush with appealing color. "You proved me wrong, Half-pint," he added softly. "You made me realize that some people *do* put legs on their faith."

"By the way," he added, "I found the missing articles."

At her puzzled frown, he explained. "The clippings from your scrapbook."

"Oh! Where were they? *What* were they?"

"Phil had them," he replied grimly. "And what they were," he said with a meaningful look, "were articles you sent your mother when you received a journalism award."

"Hm. What award?" Danni asked vaguely.

"Some kind of recognition for Christian journalists. It was for courage and special effort in investigative reporting," he said pointedly.

"Ah . . . I see," she said with a sheepish grin.

His next question sobered her quickly. "Are you—planning to stay around here to help out with all this transition at the Colony?" His words were impersonal, even casual, but Danni heard the slight catch in his voice; felt the tension in him; saw his eyes darken as their gazes met and locked.

She was only vaguely aware when Tucker cleared his throat and rose from the table, touching Add lightly on the shoulder. "Jerry, I could use some help in the barn. Want to come along?"

"Jerry?" Logan repeated.

"Yes, sir, Tucker's going to be calling me by my life—by

my first name from now on," the boy explained quietly.

"I see," Logan said with a smile. "Ah . . . Tucker?"

"Hm?" Having showered away the grime with which he'd covered himself that morning, Tucker was again neat and dignified in his crisp work shirt and jeans. His waving silver hair shone.

Logan gave him a look that was only for the two of them before saying warmly, "Many thanks, *kemo sabe*."

Tucker returned his look for an instant, then nodded and led Jerry from the cabin.

Danni and Logan sat in silence for what seemed like a very long time after Tucker and the boy closed the door behind them. Finally Logan said, "He asked me if Jerry could stay with us awhile—maybe permanently."

Danni caught her breath hopefully. "Oh, Logan—"

"I think I'd enjoy having him. He's a nice kid. And Tucker's great with teenagers, he really is. He's helped more than one get his head together. You haven't been around him enough to see it, I s'pose, but he is one wonderful Christian man. He'll bring Jerry to the Lord if anyone can."

Danni nodded. "I still can't get over the change in Add—Jerry—the way he helped you and Tucker. I wonder what made him do it."

He gave her a startled look. "Danni, that boy cares deeply for you, don't you know that? I think he'd give his own life to help you."

Her eyes misted. "I'm . . . very fortunate. To have people like Jerry and Tucker . . . and you . . . to care about me so much. I hate to think where I'd be otherwise."

"Danni—"

"Yes?" She felt slightly breathless and wondered why.

"Do you remember when you asked me why I stayed around here?"

It wasn't the question she had half-hoped for, but she tried not to let her disappointment show. "Yes."

"And I told you I loved the town, and the people—" he supplied.

"Yes, I remember. Why?"

He sighed heavily, looking away from her. "That wasn't the whole truth. I need to tell you the rest of it."

"What are you talking about, Logan?"

He drained the last drop of coffee from his cup before answering. "It's true that I love this town. But for a long time I didn't love the people. I think maybe I can now, if the Lord will help me find that forgiveness you told me I need."

Danni started to protest—that he was being too hard on himself—but he cut her off. "What kept me here wasn't love . . . it was an obssession."

He touched his index finger lightly to the little ridge where her brows knit together in a puzzled frown, smiled ruefully, then went on. "I had to prove myself, here, where it mattered most. I wanted . . . to show the whole town that a McGarey could make it." He swallowed hard, hesitating only a moment. "I wanted their acceptance. I can't remember a time when I haven't wanted it. I let you think it was something noble. It wasn't. I just had to prove myself. It was that simple."

Danni's heart overflowed as she studied his strong, yet vulnerable face. She knew what this admission must have cost him, and loved him even more than ever for his need to offer it. "Why are you telling me this, Logan?" she questioned gently.

He lifted his shoulders in a self-mocking shrug. "I don't know. Maybe it's because I'm finally beginning to understand how wrong I've been, expecting so much from other people—and myself. Maybe it made it easier for me to measure up," he said thoughtfully, "when I could tear everyone else down a little. I just . . . wanted you to know the truth. I've known the Lord personally for a long time—since high school, as a matter of fact—but I was so wrapped up in

187

anger and bitterness, I never could trust Him to work things out."

This enigma of a man had more chambers to his soul than anyone Danni had ever known. And she suspected there were still numerous unopened doors in the person of Logan McGarey.

"As long as it's confession time," he continued with a hint of a smile, "I s'pose I need to apologize for the way I yelled at you earlier today, out at the Colony."

"Yes . . . well, you certainly did put me in my place," she said, letting her bruised feelings show.

"I was scared," he said flatly. "It's one thing to mouth off about the danger of apathy," he said dryly, "but it gets a little stickier when someone you . . . care about . . . is the one putting her life on the line." He paused, then touched her cheek lightly. "I only yelled at you because I was afraid."

Not trusting her voice, Danni simply nodded.

Several moments passed without either of them speaking. When Logan finally did break the silence, his voice was little more than a whisper. "You never did answer my question."

Danni stared at him blankly.

"Are you going to stay here in Red Oak?" he asked gruffly. "What happens now that you've got your story?"

"Oh . . . well, I have to write it, of course. And I want to help out at the Colony, at least for awhile. We have to get medical care for everyone, and see what can be done to make good use of that place and—"

Suddenly, Logan stood up and walked over to the wall hook where his uniform jacket hung. Danni glanced quickly down at her plate and felt the bottom drop out of her heart. She had really thought he might be about to—well, certainly he'd given her every indication the other night that he was . . . *serious* about her. But of course he'd never actually mentioned the word. Probably she had been terribly wrong to assume that he might be thinking about marriage . . .

probably it had never entered his mind . . . probably she was more than a little foolish . . . .

It took her a minute to realize what he was doing. Logan returned to the table and pulled her to her feet, encircling one of her wrists and one of his—with a pair of handcuffs! And all the while, he continued to stare down into her face with a grave, resigned expression.

"Wh—what do you think you're doing?!"

"Arresting you," he said tonelessly, leading her over to the couch in front of the fireplace, then pulling her down beside him.

"Logan McGarey, you unlock these things right now, do you hear me? This isn't funny—"

"Breaking and entering is against the law. I have to arrest you," he said in that infuriating monotone.

"You know very well," Danni began indignantly, flustered by the closeness of his face to hers, "I had no other way to get into that infirmary—"

She couldn't move, that was the problem. Those ridiculous handcuffs had made a prisoner out of her, and trying to pull away seemed only to make it easier for him to pull her closer. "I'm not talking about the infirmary," he said evenly, watching her closely.

"Well, then, stop this foolishness about *arresting* me! You know very well you aren't going to arrest me!"

"But I already have," he insisted softly, touching her lips with his so fleetingly she might have imagined it. He gathered her with his free arm into a gentle, but secure, embrace. "You broke into my heart," he murmured against a fragrant wave of hair at her temple, "and then you walked right on in and stole it for yourself. Now, I'm just a cop, not a lawyer, but I know enough to be pretty sure that's breaking and entering. So I'm arresting you."

Danni narrowed her eyes. "I believe I'm entitled to a trial."

189

"That's true, you are," he considered. "It'll go a lot easier for you if you plea bargain."

"What kind of deal are we discussing?"

He pulled her even closer, brushing her forehead with a gentle kiss, then tucking a stray wisp of hair behind her ear. "Well, I've got a little clout with the judge. If you accept what I offer, I'm sure I can get all charges dropped."

"What are you offering?" She traced the rim of the handcuffs with one finger.

"A life sentence. In my custody."

She thought about it, but not for too long. "I think your terms are acceptable, Sheriff," she murmured, gently touching his bruised cheek with a kiss to seal their agreement.